F
RASH

Rash, Ron, 1953-

Saints at the river.

$24.00

213398

DATE			
8·04			

BAKER & TAYLOR

ALSO BY RON RASH

NOVELS
One Foot in Eden

SHORT FICTION
The Night New Jesus Fell to Earth
Casualties

POETRY
Eureka Mill
Among the Believers
Raising the Dead

SAINTS AT THE RIVER

SAINTS

AT THE

RIVER

∽

RON RASH

Henry Holt and Company
New York

Henry Holt and Company, LLC
Publishers since 1866
115 West 18th Street
New York, New York 10011

Henry Holt® is a registered trademark of
Henry Holt and Company, LLC.

Library of Congress Cataloging-in-Publication Data

Rash, Ron, 1953–
    Saints at the river / Ron Rash.—1st ed.
        p.   cm.
    ISBN 0-8050-7487-2
    1. Women photographers—Fiction.   2. Search and rescue operations—Fiction.
3. Parent and adult child—Fiction.   4. Fathers and daughters—Fiction.
5. Environmentalists—Fiction.   6. Drowning victims—Fiction.
7. South Carolina—Fiction.   I. Title.
PS3568.A698S35 2004
813'.54—dc22   2003067630

Henry Holt books are available for special promotions and
premiums. For details contact: Director, Special Markets.

First Edition 2004

DESIGNED BY KELLY S. TOO

Printed in the United States of America

1   3   5   7   9   10   8   6   4   2

For Ann

It need not blame the votary; but it may be able to praise him only conditionally, as one who acts faithfully according to his rights.

WILLIAM JAMES
"The Value of Saintliness"

SAINTS AT THE RIVER

Part One

She follows the river trail downstream, leaving behind her parents and younger brother who still eat their picnic lunch. She is twelve years old and it is her school's Easter break. Her father has taken time off from his job and they have followed the Appalachian Mountains south, stopping first in Gatlinburg, then the Smokies, and finally this river. She finds a place above a falls where the water looks shallow and slow. The river is a boundary between South Carolina and Georgia, and she wants to wade into the middle and place one foot in South Carolina and one in Georgia so she can tell her friends back in Minnesota she has been in two states at the same time.

She kicks off her sandals and enters, the water so much colder than she imagined, and quickly deeper, up to her kneecaps, surging under the smooth surface. She shivers. Fifty yards downstream a granite cliff rises two hundred feet into the air to cast this section of river into shadow. She glances back to where her parents and brother sit on the blanket. It is warmer there, the sun full upon them. She thinks about going back but is almost halfway now. She takes a step, and the water rises higher on her knees. Four more steps, she tells herself. Just four more and I'll turn back. She takes another step and the bottom she tries to set her foot on is no longer there and she is being shoved downstream and she does not panic because she is a good swimmer and has passed all of her Red Cross courses. The water shallows and her face breaks the surface and she breathes deep. She tries to turn her body so she won't hit her head on a rock and as she thinks this she's afraid for the first time and she's suddenly back underwater and hears the rush of water against her ears. She tries to hold her breath but her knee smashes against a boulder and she gasps in pain and water pours into her mouth. Then for a few moments the water pools and slows. She rises coughing up water, gasping air, her feet dragging the bottom like an anchor trying to snag waterlogged wood or rock jut and as the current quickens again she sees her family running along the shore and she knows they are shouting her name though she cannot hear them and as the current turns her she hears the falls and knows there is nothing that will keep her from it and the current quickens and quickens and another rock smashes against her knee but she hardly feels it as she snatches another breath before the river pulls her under and she feels the river fall and she falls with it as water whitens around her and she falls deep into darkness and as she rises her head scrapes against a rock ceiling and all is black and silent and she tells herself don't breathe but the need grows inside her begin-ning in the upper stomach then up through the chest and throat and as that need rises her mouth and nose open at the same time and the lungs explode in pain and then the pain is gone along with the dark as bright colors shatter around her like glass shards, and she remembers her sixth-grade science class, the gurgle of the aquarium at the back of the room that morning the teacher held a prism out the window so it might fill with color, and she has a final beautiful thought—that she is now inside that prism and knows something even the teacher does not know, that the prism's colors are voices, voices that swirl around her head like a crown, and at that moment her arms and legs she did not even know were flailing cease and she becomes part of the river.

CHAPTER 1

Ghosts.

That's what I thought of on an early-May morning as I stared at the blank computer screen, imagined this newsroom forty or fifty years ago. Certainly there would have been more noise: the steady clacking of teletypes and typewriters, the whole room hot and sweating and loud-voiced. *Bustling* would have been the word to describe it, like a giant beehive, a fumigated one, for there would be cigarette and cigar smoke bluing the air overhead like a stalled cloud. Everywhere would be men, white men, wearing rumpled suits and ties and suspenders. No bottled water or granola bars on these guys' desks.

If their ghosts ever wandered back here, they probably assumed the place had been renovated into a hospital wing, for in the second year of a new millennium the fluorescent bulbs spread an antiseptic glow. Faces were shuttered inside cubicles, and the air was smoke-free and 72 degrees year-round. Perhaps most surprising to those men would be the fact that an equal number of women, and of varying skin tones, filled the desks.

A few things had not changed. Thanks to *The Messenger*'s skinflint owner, Thomas Hudson, salaries were still low, the hours awful, and, as always, looming deadlines provided chronic doses of stress.

My managing editor, Lee Gervais, interrupted my thoughts.

"I do believe Miss Maggie Glenn is daydreaming about me," he said.

Lee leaned over my shoulder, his eyes rheumy and red-veined as they took in my blank screen. He was thirty-eight, ten years my senior, but he looked older, the flesh on his face pasty and puffy, what hair he had retreating toward the sides and back of his head. Lee wore a white short-sleeved dress shirt. The skin on the undersides of his arms was loose like an old woman's. He came from a wealthy family, and part of his softness was the result of never using his muscles for lifting anything heavier than a tennis racket or pitching wedge. The rest came from lifting too many gin and tonics.

Yes, I almost said, because I knew Lee would have preferred the newsroom of fifty years ago, a place where he could have told dirty jokes between drags on his cigarette and sips from a whiskey bottle kept in the top desk drawer.

"No, Lee. I'm just trying to get myself motivated on a Thursday morning when I'd rather be sleeping."

"I think I can help," Lee said. "How would you like a photographer's dream assignment?"

"George Clooney coming to town?" I asked.

"Better than that. A chance to work with Allen Hemphill on a sure front-page feature."

"What's the catch?"

Lee shook his head. "How did an Oconee County farm girl get so cynical?"

Lee's low-country accent made *girl* and *gull* indistinguishable. It was an accent I knew he had refined the way another man might perfect some convoluted Masonic handshake. And in a way that was what his accent was: a sign of belonging. It spoke of old money and old houses, of Porter-Gaud Academy and Charleston cotillions.

"A year of working for you," I said.

"So are you interested or not?"

"I'm interested. But why not Phil or Julian?"

"The assignment's in Oconee County. Since you know the natives, you can translate mountain speech into standard English for Hemphill."

So there is a catch, I thought.

"Contrary to what you may have heard, Lee, Oconee County's not the heart of darkness. It's four hours away, not four centuries."

I tried to smile but I'd heard such comments too many times since I'd moved to Columbia.

"Sounds about right to me," Lee said. "That part of the state used to be called Dark Corner. I suspect there's a reason."

"I can tell you the reason. Your ancestors down in Charleston were ticked off because mountain people wouldn't help fight to keep slaves."

Lee nodded. "Mountain people. Is that the correct term now? I guess the PC ayatollahs would give me twenty lashes if I said *hillbilly*."

"They should," I said, my tone no longer playful. "It's an offensive term."

Lee's act got old quickly, but he had given me good assignments in the twelve months I'd worked with him. He'd also talked Thomas Hudson into giving me a raise at Christmas. Lee wasn't a bad man, just the kind who mistook insensitivity for masculinity. He had been in Kappa Alpha at the University of Georgia, and behind his desk he'd hung a picture of his fraternity brothers on the porch of their antebellum two-story house. They were dressed as Confederate soldiers. Not mere foot soldiers, of course, but officers with swords and plumed hats. He'd always be a frat boy.

"Hey, I'm just joking," Lee said.

I smiled at him, the same way I'd smile at an eight-year-old boy.

"What will Hemphill and I be doing in Oconee County?"

"Something on the girl who drowned up there three weeks ago."

"They finally got her out?"

"No," Lee said, "and that's the story. Her father is starting to raise hell, saying the locals aren't doing enough. He's trying to get some portable dam company involved, but the tree huggers want to stop that. They're swearing on their humpback whale CDs it's against some federal law."

"The Wild and Scenic Rivers Act. It prohibits anyone from disturbing the river's natural state."

"So you already know about all this?"

"If you mean the girl, just what I've read in the paper. But I know about the Tamassee, and I probably know most of the people involved."

"Good. That's even better. I get the feeling this story is going to break national. The *Atlanta Constitution* has done a long article, and the *Charlotte Observer* has someone up there now. I've heard CNN may do something as well."

Lee glanced at the wall clock. I wondered if he was checking how long before lunchtime and a chance to down a couple of Heinekens at the Capital Grill. I occasionally joined him there, and I'd seen how his eyes closed when he raised the green bottle for his first long swallow. I knew that was probably the high point of his working day, that he must have felt like a climber at altitude getting a hit of bottled oxygen.

"The story's getting national play—is that how you were able to convince Hemphill to take it?"

"Hudson chose the assignment," Lee said, "and pushed Hemphill hard. Hudson's evidently getting tired of his highest-paid reporter covering chitlin struts and peach festivals."

"So you wanted him on it as well?"

"I'm only doing what the boss wants, following the party line. But just because he's won some hotshot awards," Lee said, frustration in his voice, "it's not like he's earned the right to take a good salary and do nothing. If he was seventy and had been doing this fifty years, okay, but Hemphill's thirty-nine for God's sake. He hasn't put in twenty years yet."

More than just frustration, I thought, when Lee finished. Perhaps professional jealousy. Perhaps resentment that someone of a lower caste had surpassed him in status.

Lee glanced at the clock again. "Give Hudson credit. If he can get Hemphill off his ass, get him to write to his capability, this could be one hell of a story. Just pray they don't get her out before that dam's built, because you'll get some good pictures, something UPI or Reuters might pick up."

"I think I'll save my prayers for a worthier cause."

"Suit yourself," Lee said, "but that girl can't get any deader than she already is. If we get a good story out of what's happening now, that's not so terrible. It's not hurting her."

He laid his hand on my shoulder.

"I need to know by twelve if you want this. Otherwise, I'll send Julian."

"Okay," I said. "I'll let you know by twelve."

His grip tightened. My Uncle Mark once told me that a man's hands reveal a lot about him. Lee's were smoother and softer than any woman's I'd grown up with.

Lee let go of my shoulder and stepped out of my cubicle.

"If you don't go, you're disappointing not just me but Hemphill."

"How so?" I asked. The question was directed at his back.

"Hemphill was the one who suggested you," Lee said, pausing before he walked away. "Since I knew you were from Oconee County it seemed perfect, so I convinced Hudson you were the best choice."

• • •

I HAD A SHOOT AT THE UNIVERSITY IN THE AFTERNOON, BUT I couldn't remember if it was at two or two-thirty, so I checked my calendar, a calendar that had no visits to Oconee County marked on it. I hadn't been back since Christmas and had no plans to return until Aunt Margaret's birthday in July, but the office party I'd attended two weeks earlier now made me reconsider. Allen and I were the only singles, so it wasn't surprising we ended up in a corner together, leaning against a wall and sipping cheap white wine from styrofoam coffee cups. We had talked about our backgrounds, which were in many ways similar—both of us growing up in the rural South, both of us the first in our families to go to college. Yet I did most of the talking. It was clear that this was a man who'd spent much of his life letting people reveal themselves to him, not vice versa.

And I was a woman who spent much of her life focusing on surfaces to reveal deeper meanings. Allen wore a wedding band, although I'd overheard Hudson's secretary say SINGLE had been checked on his insurance application. I'd glanced at that wedding ring several times, wondering if it symbolized some lingering attachment to an ex-wife. Or was it merely a prop to keep women such as myself at bay, let us know he wasn't interested?

But he was interested, at least had seemed so at the time. As the days passed and I hadn't heard from him I'd begun to second-guess my instincts. Now, however, Lee had confirmed them.

"Good girl," Lee said when I stopped by his office on my way out to lunch. "I wouldn't send you up there if I didn't know you'd do a great job."

"When do we leave?"

"Two o'clock tomorrow. That gives you plenty of time to make the meeting the Forest Service has set up."

"Tomorrow afternoon I'm supposed to photograph a Confederate flag rally."

"We getting ready to secede again?" Lee quipped. "I'd better go home and dust off my uniform."

"Why bother, Lee? You'd just lose again."

"You think so?"

I tried to imagine Lee on a battlefield in Virginia, shoeless and surviving on ditch water and hardtack. But I knew he'd have dropped dead of a heart attack before he marched across Bull Street, much less across the Georgia and Virginia state lines.

"So what about the rally?" I asked.

"I'll send Phil." Lee smiled. "This will be like a paid vacation. Just take a few photos and we'll pick up the tab. You'll even have a Pulitzer Prize finalist for a chauffeur."

I went back to my cubicle and stared at a blank screen. The only sounds in the surrounding cubicles were fingertips tapping keyboards, a mouse clicking like a telegraph key. Ten people in the room and not one talking. You would have thought human speech had become obsolete as smoke signals. I wondered how the old newspapermen would react to this muted environment. Would they be able to work without the shouting traffic of typesetters and galley boys, the background roar of presses, the smell and smear of ink?

I unsealed my coffee. Moist heat rose from the styrofoam, carrying with it the rich, dark odor that always reminded me of fresh-dug earth, not the sandy loam of the piedmont but the black mountain soil flung off shovels to open my mother's grave.

Ghosts, I told myself, more ghosts.

CHAPTER 2

To get to Tamassee, South Carolina, you leave the interstate at the last exit before the Georgia line. You turn right at the stop sign, and suddenly mountains leap up as though they'd been crouching along the four-lane waiting for the car to turn. You follow Highway 11 into Westminster and turn left on Highway 76, and all the while the mountains get bigger, narrowing the sky until the gap between clouds and earth disappears. The two-lane road coils upward like a black snake climbing a tree. Soon you notice fewer homes and mailboxes and more cornfields and barbed wire and woods. You see the dogwood trees, and it's like time-lapse photography in reverse. White blossoms that puddled the ground in Columbia re-attach themselves to the limbs, brighten the woods like crown fire. On the highest mountains, green buds still clinch the flowers. The homes, except for a few two-story farmhouses, are small A-frames and trailers. Then there are no houses at all, only curves with wooden guard posts jutting from the roadside. You pass a billboard that says LAUREL MIST: ANOTHER TONY BRYAN PLANNED COMMUNITY. Above the caption a fawn grazes on a golf course. On some of these curves you will see a cross made of wood or styrofoam. Often there is a vase or Mason jar filled with flowers, sometimes a plastic angel or pair of praying hands. Shrines that make the ascent like some Appalachian version of the stations of the cross.

"Looks like this is a dangerous road," Allen Hemphill said.

"Yes, especially during the winter."

Woods pressed close to the road on both sides now. A few weeks earlier, Judas trees would have created a scattered blush across the understory. Jessamine and silver bells would have lit up the forest as well, but now only the dogwoods bloomed.

"Have you ever been up here?" I asked.

"Once," Allen said. "My Sunday school class camped out on the Tamassee one weekend. Of course that was over twenty years ago. I'm sure a lot's changed."

"Probably not as much as you'd think."

I caught a whiff of Allen's aftershave, a kind of green, fresh smell, like lime. A good smell. *Never get involved with a man you don't like the smell of*, my Aunt Margaret always said.

I looked over at him, trying to gauge the difference between the face three feet from me and the picture on the back of *The Center Cannot Hold: Death and Life in Rwanda*. The genesis of that book had been the reporting he'd done in the mid-nineties for the *Washington Post*. Four years ago the book had been a finalist for a Pulitzer. I'd bought a copy after we met.

In the author photo Allen stared directly into the camera. *I've seen what most people can't imagine*, his eyes seemed to say, and something more, a hint of arrogance as well, as if to add, *and I'm good enough to make you see it as well*.

But he had done more than that. Allen's best passages in *Death and Life in Rwanda* accomplished what Brady's and Capa's most affecting war photography did. They didn't just make you see, they made you unable to forget what you'd seen.

"I brought your Rwanda book," I said. "I'd like you to sign it later, if you wouldn't mind."

"Sure," Allen said, but without much enthusiasm.

"It's a fine book. I read it in one sitting."

Allen glanced over at me skeptically.

"I tend to do that, start a book and not put it down."

"I'm bad about that myself," Allen said, smiling now. "When I was a kid I'd go to the library and be so oblivious I wouldn't know what time it was until the librarian started cutting off lights."

"Sometimes when I'm working that same thing happens. It's like I'm outside of time. Three hours will pass and seem like thirty minutes."

Allen nodded. "Writing used to be the same way for me."

"Used to be?" I asked.

"Used to be," Allen repeated.

It was clear he didn't want to explain further. I was reminded of the audio file Hudson had sent out after Allen had been hired, an interview with NPR the year of his Pulitzer nomination. Despite a decade out of the South, Allen's voice was pure Carolina midlands, but his manner was brisk, his answers almost sharp. At one point, when the interviewer asked if he ever questioned his ability to continue covering a particularly tough story, he seemed on the verge of losing his patience. *No*, he replied. Though any significant story had an emotional component, it was the reporter's job to redirect that emotional energy into the service of clarity. Then the interviewer asked if he planned to continue working overseas, and the tension seemed to dissolve as Allen laughed and said something to the effect that he probably would, though his wife was trying to get his passport revoked.

Evidently she, or they, had decided to get their marriage revoked instead. I wondered if it was the long overseas assignments that had ended the marriage. Or, perhaps, problems with the "emotional component." I glanced at his wedding ring and remembered a poem from my British Lit class where a woman wore a necklace engraved with the words *Noli me tangere*. Touch me not.

The blacktop curved a final time. WASHED IN THE BLOOD OF THE LAMB proclaimed a graying piece of wood nailed to a tree. A few yards beyond was another wooden sign with DAMASCUS PENTECOSTAL CHURCH and an arrow pointing left. Once the two-lane straightened, apple orchards lined the road and then a wide-porched building with WHITEWATER RAFTING TOURS painted on the slanting roof came into view. Thirty yards beyond was Billy Watson's service station and general store.

"We're low on gas," I said, nodding at the fuel gauge. "This is the only place to get some this side of the river."

"I hadn't noticed," Allen said, and flicked on the blinker with his left hand.

MINNOWS AND REDWORMS FOR SALE, the hand-printed placard beside the pumps read.

"The pumps aren't on," I said. "You have to pay first."

Though it was still too early for many tourists, Billy sat in a rocking chair on his store's rickety porch, a book in his hand and a brown Labrador retriever at his feet. He wore a torn flannel shirt and faded overalls. A black beard draped off his chin like Spanish moss. All his costume lacked was a corncob pipe. Billy had a degree in agriculture from Clemson University, and his family owned the biggest apple orchard in the valley, but he'd decided after college that his true calling was playing Snuffy Smith to fleece tourists. He swore if he could find a cross-eyed boy who could play banjo, he'd stick that kid on the porch and increase his business 25 percent.

"Maggie," Billy said. He raised his hand in greeting but did not lay his book on the banister until we'd stepped on the porch.

"This is Allen Hemphill," I said after Billy had released me from a bear hug.

"William Watson the Third," Billy said, holding his hand out. "But you can call me Billy since you're with Maggie."

"Nice to meet you. I'll take fifteen dollars of unleaded," Allen said, handing Billy a credit card with one hand and shaking with the other.

We stepped into the store. Even in midafternoon the two bare bulbs hanging overhead couldn't disperse the dark that pooled in the corners and lined the back wall. Billy had made changes since he'd bought the place from Lou Henson. He'd hung a hornet's nest and a tanned timber rattlesnake skin on the wall. In the back corner he'd installed a potbelly stove many tourists believed was a moonshine still.

Billy also sold items that Lou Henson never allowed on his shelves: for the tourists, T-shirts and ball caps with TAMASSEE RIVER printed across them, walking sticks, postcards; for the river rats, Tevas and Patagonia shirts, plastic dry bags for cigarettes, even a few paddles in the back.

But other parts of the store remained unchanged. The floors still smelled of linseed oil. A ceiling fan big as an airplane propeller creaked and rattled overhead. Fishing and hunting equipment crowded the first row of shelves, much of it covered by a fine layer of dust. I knew if I lifted the lid of the red battered-metal drink box Cokes and Nehis and Cheerwines would be up to their necks in ice and water so cold you had to snatch them out.

And the cigarettes. They were behind the counter, the same place they'd been eighteen years ago when my father left my brother Ben and me alone with a pot of simmering navy beans so he might come to this store and buy a pack of Camels.

I looked down and saw that my left hand lay over the part of my forearm scalded that long-ago evening. Covering the scar had been a habit I'd formed in middle school, a habit I'd never been able to break.

Allen turned from the counter.

"I'm going to get a couple of things I forgot to pack," he said, tucking the credit card back in his billfold. "If that's all right with you."

"I'm in no hurry," I said.

Billy wrote something on a receipt and placed it in the cash register. Despite the ZZ Top beard, he was a handsome man, eyes a deep blue, hair the shiny black you see on a raven's wing. You didn't need the Watson family Bible to know that a few generations back Cherokee and Celt in this valley had done more than just trade and fight.

"You got any idea where Aunt Margaret is?" I asked Billy. "I called her last night but didn't get an answer."

"Joel said she went down to Greenville to see that grand-baby."

"Did he say when she'd be back?"

"No, but she'll be here in time for the singing tomorrow night. She doesn't miss those, even for a grandbaby."

Billy looked toward the back aisle where Allen lingered.

"So what brings you all up here?" he asked me.

"That girl's drowning."

Billy pointed to the hornet's nest behind him.

"That nest is nothing compared to the one stirred up since it happened, but I guess your daddy's already told you that."

"We haven't talked in a while," I said.

Billy's eyes registered disappointment but little surprise. We'd grown up on adjoining farms. As children, Billy and Ben and I had built secret clubhouses in the woods and seined for

minnows in Licklog Creek. On rainy days we played Monop-
oly and Chinese checkers. Sometimes my cousin Joel would
play too, but it was usually just us three. Momma called us
the Three Musketeers. Billy and I had stayed close through
high school and college at Clemson.

"What exactly happened to that girl?" I asked.

Allen clutched a toothbrush and toothpaste in his hand, but
he lingered in the aisle, pretending to check out the fishing
equipment.

"What I know is she was picnicking with her family and
decided to go wading," Billy said, "above Wolf Cliff Falls, of
all places."

"Did her parents try to help once she got in trouble?"

"Her mother dove into the pool three times. She's lucky
the hydraulic didn't shove her under that rock as well."

"What's a hydraulic?" Allen asked, coming up the aisle to
stand beside me. He placed the toothbrush and toothpaste on
the counter.

"A place where an obstacle makes water move in a circular
motion," I said. "It's kind of like being inside a washing
machine."

"Except in this case it's a washing machine to the tenth
power," Billy added.

"But she's not in the hydraulic?" Allen asked.

"No," Billy said. "She's behind it."

When Allen opened his billfold, I noticed the plastic photo
covers were empty.

"That comes to four dollars and thirty-two cents by my
ciphering," Billy said, taking Allen's five-dollar bill.

"So she's under that big rock on the left side of the falls?" I asked.

"That's my understanding. Randy took an underwater camera down there last week. The current makes it hard to see, but the people who looked at the film claimed they saw a body."

Billy handed Allen his change.

"But the father didn't go in the water?" Allen asked.

Billy nodded.

"Maggie here can tell you it would have been not just dangerous but useless. That water's pouring in at two hundred cubic feet a second. It would be like pulling someone out of the eye of a tornado."

"But the father wouldn't have known that she was on the other side of a hydraulic," Allen said.

Billy bit his lower lip and slowly shook his head. "I hadn't thought about that." He closed his cash register. "I reckon you-all will be at the meeting?"

"Yes," I said.

"Well, I'll look for you. It should be entertaining, depending on who shows up." Billy met my eyes. "Especially if one of them is Luke."

"Rest assured Luke will be there," I said, as the three of us stepped onto the porch.

I picked up the thick hardback on the banister, *The North American Cougar and Its Habitat* printed on the spine, and showed the title to Allen.

"When we were kids Billy thought he saw a cougar. He's been trying to prove it to the rest of us ever since."

"I did see it," Billy said. "Black-tipped tail and all."

"You don't think they're up here?" Allen asked me.

"I'm an agnostic on that question. There have been sightings for decades, but no one ever finds a carcass or scat. Luke, the guy we just mentioned, he's never seen one, and he spends more time on the river than anyone."

"The Tamassee and its watershed can hide a lot," Billy said, "even from Luke Miller. And I may have found some empirical evidence for you skeptics. My boys and me were camping on Sassafras Mountain six weeks ago and found a six-point buck. The throat had been punctured and it had been covered with leaves and branches."

"Couldn't a wild dog or bobcat do that?" I asked.

"Possibly. But here's the kicker. It had been dragged thirty yards uphill from the kill site. We're talking about maybe a two-hundred-pound deer."

"I hope you had your camera with you."

"Oh yeah. I took two rolls' worth, and I've sent copies to the folks at Fish and Wildlife."

"Heard anything back?"

"Not yet."

Allen checked his watch. "I'm going to pump the gas," he said.

Billy motioned for me to stay as Allen turned and walked to the car.

"You heard from Ben lately?" he asked.

"Last week."

"He's doing okay?"

"The baby still isn't sleeping through the night, but otherwise everything's fine."

"Tell him I said hello next time you two talk."

Billy turned his eyes from me and gazed toward Sassafras Mountain. Years back, Ben and Billy and I had climbed Sassafras. The climb had been Billy's idea, a way of getting Ben out of his room after another skin graft. At the top we'd used Billy's jackknife to carve our initials and a date into the white oak.

Allen put the handle back on the gas pump.

"I'd better go."

"Come back more often, Maggie," Billy said softly. "Your daddy's going to need you."

Billy watched from the porch as we drove away toward the river. The road was all slants and curves now. A pickup coming from the other direction swung wide on a curve, briefly crossing onto our side of the center stripe. I caught the blur of an unwhiskered face, some teen, probably still in high school.

"The way the land's slanting we must be near the river," Allen said.

"Yes," I said. "We're close now."

I looked out the passenger window. Trees thickened, some dogwoods but mainly birch and yellow poplar. TRUCKS USE LOW GEAR, a yellow sign warned. We soon passed Laurel Mist development, a guardhouse with a wooden swinging gate at the entrance.

"Are they keeping people out or in?" Allen asked.

"Out," I said, "unless you've got a whole lot of money."

We drove by apple stands. Four months from now the ground in front of them would be a bumpy red, green, and yellow quilt of Winesap, Granny Smith, and Golden Delicious.

The wood shelves would sag with gallon jugs of cider and quart jars of apple butter. Tackle boxes on the counters would fill with bills and coins. But now the stands were empty, like booths left behind by a passing carnival.

"Where does your father live?" Allen asked.

"We passed the turnoff two miles ago."

"Do you want to turn around?" Allen asked.

"No, the motel is straight ahead."

I glanced at the clock on the dash.

"The meeting's in an hour. There's a barbecue joint across from the motel. The food's great if you don't mind raising your cholesterol level ten points."

"Don't mind it a bit," Allen said. "Greasy food and sweet tea were the two things I missed most when I was up north. I've got some culinary catching up to do."

"Well, Mama Tilson's is your place, then," I said. "Nothing to eat that's not dripping in grease."

We passed Luke's log cabin, the TAMASSEE RIVER PHOTOG-RAPHY sign out front punctuated with a couple of new bullet holes that hadn't been there in December. A battered aluminum canoe lay upside down on the porch. Luke's pickup wasn't parked out front. I wondered if he was already at the community center.

"Here," I said, and Allen turned into the Tamassee Motel's gravel driveway.

"I'll be at Mama Tilson's," I said, as he unlocked the trunk. "Come on over when you get settled in."

"What about your check-in?"

"I'm staying at my father's house. I'll drive out there after the meeting, unless you need the car."

I leaned into the trunk and gripped the handle of the laptop. Allen placed his left hand on my wrist.

"I can get it all myself," he said, letting his palm glide lightly onto the back of my hand and pause there a moment as his grip replaced mine. I felt the smooth center of the palm, the tougher skin where fingers and palm connected.

Allen lifted his suitcase and computer from the trunk.

"No, I won't need the car." He set down the suitcase. "Here," he said, and handed me the keys.

"See you in a few minutes," I said.

I watched him walk across the asphalt and into the office. He was a good-looking man, his eyes that deep, steady blue you see in an October sky, his wavy brown hair starting to gray at the edges. His haircut was functional: barbershop, not salon. He had a hard lean body that would look good in jeans and a T-shirt. He kept himself in shape.

Perhaps it was just the longing of a woman who hadn't been with a man in over a year, but as I watched him disappear through the doorway I wondered what the fingertips and palm of his hand would feel like pressed to the small of my back. *Maggie Glenn, you've been a long time lonely*, I said to myself, and drove across the road.

"LOOK WHAT THE CAT'S DRAGGED IN," MAMA TILSON announced, bustling out from behind the counter, her body covered by the white barbecue-stained hospital gown she always wore instead of an apron. She leaned forward to hug me, not letting the gown touch my clothes. "Good to see you, girl."

She stepped back and looked me over. "You're just as pretty as ever. I still tell Billy Watson and those Moseley boys the biggest mistake they ever made was letting you get away."

"I hope you don't say that in front of their wives."

"Of course I do," Mama Tilson said. "Their wives know well as I do it's the gospel truth."

Mama Tilson's son Ely opened the screen door next to the counter. He'd been tending the barbecue pit and sweat beaded his forehead.

"This hog's ready to baste," he said.

"Okay," Mama Tilson said. "You go have a seat, Maggie. I'll be with you in a minute."

"No rush," I said. "I've got a friend joining me."

"This friend wouldn't happen to be a man by any chance?"

"He's just someone I work with."

Mama Tilson laughed. "Well, Maggie, your face all ablush argues otherwise, but I won't pry. You just let me or Becky know when you and that friend of yours are ready to order."

I had my choice of where to sit, though the room would fill quickly when people started getting off work. Stools lined the counter and picnic tables filled the room's center. The barbecue pit was right outside the screen door, and a pungent mix of hickory smoke, vinegar, and cooked pork drifted in through the screen. I walked to the back where booths lined the wall and sat down. Unlike Billy's store, nothing had changed here except the date on the wall calendar. I let my gaze linger on the battered metal cash register, the stools repaired with duct tape, and the Wurlitzer jukebox that played decades-old 45s.

I could frame all of it—cash register, stools, and jukebox—into one photograph and create the kind of picture you find in a doctor's office or on a wall calendar because it invokes a supposedly simpler time and place. A picture that, were I to send it to him, would hang in a prominent place in my brother Ben's house. A picture he'd point to fondly and explain its place in his past to friends and in-laws.

The last time we talked, Ben had spoken of bike trips and nights camping out with Billy in the backyard. Listening to him, you would have thought he'd gone through childhood with nothing worse happening to him than a stubbed toe. Someone who didn't know him well would say he was merely in denial, but I did know Ben well, and I knew the life he'd made for himself as a man. The early history of his life was like history written in chalk on a blackboard—something he could smudge and then erase through sheer good-heartedness.

But I wasn't like my brother. I couldn't let things go. I didn't even want to. Forgetting, like forgiving, only blurred things. Even Ben, for all his nostalgia, had put the whole width of the United States between him and South Carolina.

"So what's good?" Allen said, as he sat down and opened the menu.

"The special."

"I don't see it," Allen said.

"It's not on the menu," I said. "You have to ask. Only locals are worthy of the special. But since you're with me you can order it."

"Well, I wouldn't want to miss out on a once-in-a-lifetime opportunity."

Becky, Mama Tilson's daughter-in-law, came to take our order.

"Two specials," Allen said.

"Hush puppies or rolls?" Becky asked.

"Hush puppies," Allen said.

"And what to drink?"

"Sweet tea."

Becky left to get our drinks.

"How'd I do?" Allen asked.

"She's got you nailed as a downstate sand lapper."

"What gave me away?"

"The sweet tea."

"How so?"

"That adjective doesn't exist at Mama Tilson's. It's not tea unless it is sweetened. Saying sweet tea here is like asking for pork barbecue."

"But I was doing well up until then?"

"Pretty good," I said. "Though you didn't tell her if you wanted apple or peach cobbler."

"Which one was I supposed to say?"

"Apple. A county boy is going to pick what he—or at least a good many of his neighbors—make a living from."

The picnic tables began to fill with families, and though I

didn't know all the children's first names I knew the names of their parents and grandparents.

Earl Wilkinson came in as well and picked up something to go. Earl was a local who'd made good selling rafting trips to business and church groups and anybody else who would pay his fee and sign a waiver. He'd started off with one raft and himself the only guide. Now he had a flotilla of rafts and, during the peak season, several dozen employees. As I watched Earl walk out the door I wondered whose side he'd take at the meeting.

"Time to give you some background on the Tamassee," I said when Becky brought our tea. "If I don't, you'll have no idea what they're yelling at each other about tonight."

"I'm listening," Allen said.

"The most important thing is that the Tamassee is a Wild and Scenic River. That means it's against federal law to disturb the river's natural state. A lot of what this is going to come down to is how much change, if any, in the river's environment can be made. That includes temporary trails, portable dams, and anything else that's not already there."

"But all those things are just for short-term use."

"The environmentalists, especially Luke Miller, won't see it that way. They believe that once you let the law be violated, you open the Tamassee up for all sorts of other exceptions, including ones for developers. And that's not just an overreaction. I've seen it happen. Twenty years ago the Chattahoochee was as pristine as the Tamassee. Now that watershed's little more than a housing development with an open sewer running through its middle."

"Sounds like you may have already made up your mind about whose side you're on," Allen said, but his tone made it unclear if he thought that a good or bad thing.

"Maybe I have. It's nice to know there's something in the world that's uncorrupted. Something that can't be bought and cut up into pieces so somebody can make money off it."

Allen smiled. "I didn't realize I'd be eating dinner with Wendell Berry."

"Sorry to wax poetic," I said, "but the Tamassee's the last free-flowing river in this state. A wild river's something that can't be replicated or brought back once it's gone."

Becky wove through the kids and picnic tables with our food.

"Anything else you need?" Becky said, as she laid our plates before us.

"We'd like apple cobbler for our dessert," Allen said.

"You got it," Becky said.

Allen stared at a plate filled with sliced barbecue, baked beans, hush puppies, and cole slaw.

"It's not mustard-based."

"Of course it isn't," I said. "Up here we know mustard is for turkey sandwiches, though some of the old folks do use it as a chest salve."

"What flavors it, then?"

"Vinegar. That and hickory smoke." I nodded at his plate. "Try it. Then try to tell me with a straight face it's not the best barbecue you've ever tasted."

Allen raised a small portion to his mouth, then a larger one. "I may have to rethink my views on barbecue," he said.

Maybe it was the food or just the chance to relax after driving four hours, but Allen was talkative. He told me about his newspaper work in Georgia and Virginia before the *Washington Post* had hired him eleven years ago.

"What was it like growing up in Chester?" I asked, trying to get something out of him less tied to work.

"Probably pretty much like growing up here, the only difference being the mountains. There was the mill, but not much else. I did my share of hunting and traipsing in the woods. I fished and swam in a river. A good place to grow up, though when I was eight years old I already knew I'd leave."

"How did you know that?"

"My third-grade teacher had one of those maps that flattens out the whole world. It was so big it covered half a wall. On the first day of class she took a pin and stuck it on the map. This is how big Chester is compared to the rest of the world, she'd said. Then she stuck a thumbtack where the pin had been. That's South Carolina, she'd said. I knew right then I'd have to know more of the world than what a pin or thumbtack could cover."

Becky replaced our plates with bowls of cobbler. I looked around and saw more familiar faces. Kids roamed the room while their parents talked between tables. Hank Williams wailed on the Wurlitzer. Friday night in Tamassee, South Carolina, the pinprick where I'd been born and raised. It wasn't much, but it was what almost all the kids I'd grown up with had settled for. They had their own kids now and their blue-collar jobs and mortgages, and this was what passed as a luxury, one night a week eating out and some Saturday night music at Billy's store. But as I looked around the room at several people I'd gone to school with, they seemed, at least tonight, satisfied with their lives.

"So when you were a child did you know you'd leave here?" Allen asked.

"Yes."

"Do you ever think about coming back here to live?"

"No."

"Why not?"

"It would be too hard to fit back in, especially since I didn't fit in all that well when I was here."

"I can understand that," Allen said.

Allen's hands and forearms were on the table. As he spoke, he closed his left hand and pressed it into his right palm, covering the wedding ring.

"How do you know so much about the Tamassee? Did you spend a lot of time on it as a kid?"

"Some. But most of what I know I learned later."

"How was that?" Allen asked, his right palm still covering the ring.

So I told how about Saturday mornings at the community center when I'd helped Luke and the others he'd gathered to win the Tamassee its Wild and Scenic River status. How the following summer I'd worked as a photographer on the river, taking pictures of rafters. I explained about working with Luke, who knew the Tamassee better than anyone else on the planet. I told Allen about cool, dewy mornings when we launched at Canaan Sluice and paddled down to Five Falls, our day spent taking action shots of the rafters. I described evenings we were alone on the river after the tourists and other guides had left, just Luke and me in a canoe as the sun fell behind Sassafras Mountain and the only sounds were the river and an occasional bullfrog.

"Sounds like Huck and Jim," Allen said.

"Yes, but a little more than friendship, at least for a while."

A smile creased Allen's lips. Something else flickered across his face as well—curiosity.

"I see," he said. "You think he'd talk to me?"

"Yes, if you mean about the river."

"The river," Allen said, his smile widening before he filled his mouth with the last spoonful of cobbler. "But who knows what other topics might come up."

He checked his watch.

"Time to go," he said.

A TRACTOR WAS PLOWING THE FIELD BEHIND MAMA TILSON'S, and when we stepped out into the parking lot I smelled the rich open-earth odor of a fresh-turned field, a smell I always associated with spring but not necessarily the planting of new life.

It had been raining on the morning we gathered under the green Jenkins Funeral Home tent to bury my mother. The tent hadn't been big enough, and we huddled so close to the coffin and the grave it seemed we were crowding Momma out of her own funeral. Especially Daddy—the way he stood next to Preacher Tilson, saying amen after each passage, reading from the Bible himself after Preacher Tilson finished and telling Aunt Margaret what hymn to sing. Then, as we walked back out into a day gray as the gravestones, Daddy told Preacher Tilson it was finally over and what a blessing that was. I marveled at how even at the moment when all five of us could hear the rasp of shovels, the dry splash of dirt against the varnished wood, he couldn't acknowledge we'd never hear Momma's voice again, couldn't realize that the best way to honor Momma's silence was not to speak but instead to listen to the sound of the shovels gathering dirt and the dirt hitting the wood and, all around that, the steady hush of the rain. The rest of us realized it but Daddy didn't. He kept on talking, all the way to the car.

I knew something else as we moved through that stone maze the dead had placed between us and the rest of our lives: It wasn't only Daddy I was angry with but Momma as well. Because now I was left to set things right between us. Momma had surely sensed my anger as well, because she could always intuit things like that in a way Daddy never had. She may have even believed my resentment was about having to nurse her those weekends, that I was twenty years old and wanted my Friday and Saturday nights for something other than helping my mother die. She'd never asked about the anger, never acknowledged it. But that was how it had always been. Silence then and silence now.

CHAPTER 3

The Tamassee Community Center was little more than cinder blocks, tables, and a few dozen metal folding chairs. The roof needed new shingles, and the one window had a piece of plywood where a pane had been. Hawkweed and broom sedge sprouted thick around the edges, some of the plants sortieing out to rise in the gravel parking lot. People voted in this building and occasionally a revival or gospel sing would be held, but passersby would most likely take it as a boarded-up honky-tonk.

But not tonight. The parking lot was full, mainly with pickups. Luke's battered blue Ford Ranger was among them, on its back window a faded decal with EARTH FIRST printed beneath an upraised fist. I did not see my father's truck, and that in itself said a lot about how sick he was. He was a man who'd want to have his say in this matter.

Allen pulled off on the roadside behind a Jaguar.

"That car looks out of place. You know who it belongs to?"

"Nobody I know," I said. "Maybe some big-shot reporter. Definitely not a photographer."

"I'd say more likely a newspaper owner," Allen said, picking up the pocket tape recorder that lay beside my camera.

Inside, people already stood against the walls, but there were two empty chairs in the last row next to Billy.

"Saving those seats for somebody, Billy?" I asked.

"None other than your own lovely self," he said, "and of course your companion."

I stashed the Nikon and backpack under my chair, looked for Luke, and found him in the front row. His face was tan, as it was year-round, because no matter how cold or high the river, he ran it almost every day. He wore a flannel shirt, blue jeans, gray wool socks, and Tevas. Knowing Luke, the shirt was probably the same one he'd worn eight years earlier when we'd gathered in this same building.

From the beginning, I had known Luke was interested in me—from the way his eyes often found mine when he spoke to the whole group, the way he lingered by the table where I worked, how he began to come to Henson's Store on Saturday nights and always seemed to end up talking to me more than anyone else there. Apparently his interest had been obvious to others as well. I'd look up and catch Daddy watching us, and he was never smiling.

One Sunday afternoon Luke came out to the house. Daddy got to the front door before I could, still wearing his dark pants and white dress shirt. He'd taken off his cuff links and rolled up the sleeves, revealing two forearms muscled by decades of lifting and hauling.

"Maggie asked to borrow this book so I thought I'd bring it over," Luke said, holding out a copy of *The Clearcutting of Paradise*.

Daddy took the book from Luke's hand and held it with his thumb and forefinger a few moments as if weighing it. "What do you reckon this book's made of, son?"

Luke smiled slightly. "I get your point, Mr. Glenn. But there's a difference between clearcutting and responsible timber harvesting."

"I've been cutting pulpwood since I was twelve years old," Daddy replied. "I don't do it full-time like Harley, but there's been lean times when pulpwood money was all that got the bills paid."

"I respect that," Luke said.

"No, you don't," Daddy said. "If you did you wouldn't be trying to put people like Harley out of work."

He handed the book back to Luke.

"Maggie don't need to read this," Daddy said.

I moved closer to the door, close enough that Luke could see me. But his eyes were on Daddy, not me.

"I'd appreciate it if you'd give it to her anyway, Mr. Glenn," Luke said.

Daddy closed the door in Luke's face.

"You didn't have a reason to treat him like that," I said, as Luke's pickup bumped back down the drive. "He just wanted to share a book."

I kept my voice low because Momma was sleeping.

"He's been up here not even a year and wants to tell us how to live," Daddy said. "What we can do and not do, when Glenns and Winchesters have been in this valley two hundred years."

Daddy looked at me, the anger clear on his face if not in the volume of his voice.

"And you supporting them," Daddy said. "If that's what going to college does to you, I ought not have let you go in the first place."

"You didn't let me go," I said. "I went, and with no help from you. I wouldn't be there if I didn't have a scholarship."

"No help but eighteen years of clothing and feeding you," Daddy said. "Keeping a roof over your head. And it didn't seem to make no difference to you when it was pulpwood money that bought your back-to-school clothes and paid the grocery and doctor bills."

"Maybe there wouldn't have been so many doctor bills if you hadn't needed a pack of cigarettes so bad."

Daddy didn't say anything for a few seconds. The anger that tensed his features became something harder to define, more unsettling.

Momma coughed in the back room. I could hear the mattress springs as she shifted in the bed.

"I ain't letting you take my truck to no more of those meetings," he finally said.

"I'll get a ride with Billy then," I said, "and if he isn't going I'll walk."

"I'll not burden your mother with this," Daddy said, his teeth clinched to keep his voice low. "She's got enough to handle without knowing you're siding against the very people you've grown up among."

And that made me madder, his bringing Momma into it, because Momma had never mattered before when we'd had our fights. She'd never allowed herself to matter. What remorse I might have felt about my hospital bill comment slipped away like smoke.

"That's not what I'm doing," I said. "No more than Billy or Earl Wilkinson are."

"That is what you're doing," Daddy said, "and them others as well."

"You're just too ignorant to understand," I said, and in my mind I saw another layer added to the wall we'd created between us.

"Ignorant," Daddy said, and shook his head. He said it again, the same way a child at a spelling bee repeats a word. "My daddy made me quit school at fifteen. Hired me out to Harley Winchester's daddy like I was no more than a mule or draft horse. Old Man Winchester worked me like one too, ten hours a day, and every dime I made went in my daddy's pocket. I've given you more than my daddy ever gave me. If I'm ignorant it's because I never got the chances you got."

We didn't say anything else. Everything we could hurt each other with we'd said. So Daddy and I just stood there, silent, like boxers who have thrown their best punches and found their opponent still standing.

"I GOT AN ANSWER TO WHY THE FATHER DIDN'T DIVE IN," BILLY said, pointing to the far wall where Sheriff Cantrell and his deputy, Hubert McClure, watched the crowd. "Our esteemed deputy came by the store as I was closing up. Turns out Herb Kowalsky had about as good a reason not to get into a river as you can have."

"And what's that?"

"He can't swim."

"Yes, that explains it," Allen said, more to himself than Billy and me. I hadn't even known he was listening. He turned his attention back to rewinding the tape in his pocket recorder.

"His wife and kids had been after him for years to learn. His daughter was Red Cross certified and wanted to teach him herself. How's that for irony?"

Billy looked across the rows of chairs to the front, where a young man I didn't recognize placed a lectern on a metal fold-out table. The man at the lectern pulled some papers from his pockets. He wore a Forest Service uniform, on his pocket a silver name tag I couldn't read.

"Who is that?" I asked Billy.

"Walter Phillips. He's the new district ranger."

"What happened to Will McDowell?"

"Retired in February."

"Where's Phillips from?"

"Louisiana."

Two other men, both dressed in suits, walked over to Phillips. Phillips listened as the men spoke.

"Lucky guy, ain't he?" Billy said. "Your first head ranger assignment and right off you're dealing with something like this. I bet he's already wishing he was back on a bayou chasing gator poachers."

I looked at Phillips more closely. He wasn't nearly as big as Will McDowell, probably no more than five-eight and with a slim build. That would make his job harder up here, perhaps already had. There would be men, especially the loggers, who would test him more than they had McDowell. They would want to see how quickly Phillips would show weakness by falling back on his gun and badge for protection. When he did, they would know he was afraid and they would have no respect for him after that.

"Who are the men up there with him?"

"The guy in the brown coat I don't know. The other is Herb Kowalsky."

I looked at Allen. He studied the people who filled the room. You could tell he was making mental notes of what they wore, the expressions on their faces, the way they appeared to align themselves by where they stood or sat. An intensity I'd not seen in his face before marked his features, and there was something of the confidence and detachment I'd seen on the book jacket. Then the expression evaporated as quickly as it surfaced, as if he'd caught himself engaged in a habit not yet totally broken.

Walter Phillips stepped behind the lectern. For a few seconds he said nothing, just stared at his right hand as if waiting for someone to fill it with a gavel, because there were already some heated voices in the room he'd have to quiet. If Phillips was like most rangers, this must have appeared to be a dream appointment: a Wild and Scenic River, mountains, low population density. He probably hadn't believed his luck when he'd gotten this assignment, especially young as he was. Right now he seemed anything but thrilled to be district ranger of Oconee National Forest. Phillips looked like a man who'd wandered into a minefield without a map.

He finally nodded at Myra Burrell, who'd been Will McDowell's secretary and now worked for Phillips. She had a pen and notebook in her hand. His words were so soft people in the back didn't hear him.

"My name is Walter Phillips," he said, louder this time, loud enough to quiet the other voices. He looked at a sheet of paper that lay on the lectern and began to read. "I'm district ranger for the Oconee National Forest. The purpose of this meeting is to get community input concerning possible ways to recover the body of Ruth Kowalsky from the Tamassee River."

For the first time since he'd said his name, Walter Phillips looked up. His round, boyish face was flushed, and though the room wasn't particularly warm, sweat darkened his armpits and the edge of his collar. He wore a mustache, no doubt to look older, but the hair was blond and wispy. You could bet he still got carded when he bought alcohol.

"It seems only right that the first person to speak should be Herb Kowalsky, Ruth's father."

Herb Kowalsky left the front row. He looked around fifty,

his gray hair cropped close to his scalp. Low and tight, my brother Ben would have called that haircut, and it fit Kowalsky, for he had the demeanor of a former military man. He wore a dark, stylish suit you could tell had been tailor cut. He wasn't much bigger than Phillips, but he walked with the confidence of a man who expected to dominate any situation. He stepped behind the lectern and took a few moments to look the crowd over. You could tell he was used to speaking to people, even more used to people listening, which was to be expected of a man who was vice president of Minnesota's largest savings and loan.

"I want to thank Mr. Phillips for calling this meeting," he said in an accent more urban Northeast than Midwest. "I'd have liked it called sooner, but there's no reason to go into that now."

I glanced at Allen to see if he was taking notes. He wasn't, but the tape recorder's red light was on. He'd placed his palm in front of the recorder, as if to conceal it.

"The point is this," Herb Kowalsky said. "I've tried it Oconee County's way for three weeks. This county's search-and-rescue squad, this county's divers."

Kowalsky looked in the back corner where Randy and Ronny Moseley stood, TAMASSEE SEARCH AND RESCUE SQUAD printed on the front of the faded ball caps they wore. They were twins, though not identical. Ronny was six feet tall and long-limbed. He'd been a good baseball pitcher, good enough to get college scholarship offers, but, like his brother, he'd chosen instead to work in his family's orchards. Randy was similarly built, though not as tall or athletic. While his twin played baseball, Randy had learned to scuba dive. He was still in high school when he began helping recover bodies for the Search and Rescue Squad. Even then people said he was the best diver in the county.

"I was told Ruth would be out of that river in a day. Then it was a week. It rains and I'm told it's too dangerous, and two more weeks pass. I think it's time you people backed off and let the experts take over."

"Quite the diplomat, ain't he?" Billy said, not bothering to lower his voice.

I looked at Randy and Ronny, their caps creased in the middle and pushed back at the same angle, arms crossed right over left. Their faces, brown already from weeks in the orchards, revealed nothing as they stared back at Herb Kowalsky.

But the face of the man who stood beside them did. That man was my first cousin Joel Lusk, Aunt Margaret's youngest son. His arms were also crossed. Biting his lower lip with his front teeth, he shook his head slightly. Joel was twenty-nine and divorced. He lived in a trailer he'd put beside Aunt Margaret's house.

"The man I brought here with me tonight, Pete Brennon, builds portable dams," Herb Kowalsky continued. "He can divert enough water from Wolf Cliff Falls to get Ruth out, and that dam can be put up in four hours."

Kowalsky shifted his gaze to Luke.

"I'm not going to get up here and jerk you around emotionally. I could do that. I could tell you how I feel about knowing my daughter is in that river. I could have brought my wife, Ruth's mother, and let her tell you the hell these last three weeks have been. It wouldn't be hard for her to get up here and cry because that's all she's done lately. But I'm not going to put her through that. All I'm going to do is ask you to think about what you'd do if Ruth was your daughter."

Kowalsky stepped to the side of the lectern.

"Come on up here, Pete."

The man who'd been sitting next to Herb Kowalsky earlier stepped to the lectern. He looked to be in his late forties, six feet tall but paunchy. Brennon's mismatched coat and tie looked like they'd been bought a decade earlier at Kmart. He wore black-rimmed glasses that made his eyes large and owlish. If you had seen him on the street you'd have guessed pharmacist or jeweler before dam builder.

"I've already met some of you," he said, "but for those I haven't, my name is Peter Brennon. I'm the owner of Brennon Portable Dam Company in Carbondale, Illinois. I'm also the inventor of this dam."

Brennon's voice had the same flat midwestern inflection of news anchors. It was the inflection taught in Charlotte and Atlanta—even in Columbia—to Southerners ashamed of talking like their parents and grandparents. But such classes weren't taught in Oconee County.

"Mr. Kowalsky wanted me to tell you about the dam and then answer any questions."

Brennon turned his head toward Kowalsky, who had not sat down but stood next to Walter Phillips. Nonverbal communication, my college speech teacher would have called it. Kowalsky was letting Phillips and everyone else in the room know he considered this his meeting.

"Take what time you need to explain it, Pete," Kowalsky said, looking at the audience as he spoke. "There's been a lot of misinformation put out about this dam, and it's time to clear things up."

"The main idea is not to stop water but divert it to the right side of the falls," Brennon said. "The dam itself will be five feet high and fifty feet wide. It's portable. We'll put it up and take it down the same day."

Peter Brennon had placed a large laminated photograph against the podium before speaking. Now he pointed to the picture of the dam, explaining in detail how and why it would work. He spoke like an engineer—not a businessman or an advocate for a grieving family—an engineer who believed he had the solution to a challenging technical problem.

There was movement in the front row. Luke stood up, placed his hands in his front pockets, and waited for Brennon to acknowledge him.

"Make sure your machine's recording," I murmured to Allen, "because this is about to get interesting."

NO ONE STOOD UP WITH LUKE, BUT HIS SUPPORTERS FILLED THE first row. Like Luke they wore flannel shirts and jeans and river sandals. Most were college students who'd driven here just for this meeting, students who worked summers on the river. Earl Wilkinson provided them lodging and meals and as little pay as he could legally get away with.

A lot of them would have worked for free. Running white water all day and partying at night was a pretty good way to pass a summer. Any cash they pocketed was a perk. Though most of their customers saw the Tamassee as little more than a longer, more dangerous version of rides at Six Flags or Disney World, the guides considered the river sacred, and it was inevitable they'd be drawn to Luke and his cause. They called themselves river rats. "Luke's disciples," the locals called them, and seldom fondly.

I studied the girl who sat beside Luke. She wore her blond hair in a ponytail. Her hand reached out and squeezed Luke's for a moment. She turned and I got a better look. The unlined face confirmed she was still in her early twenties, which was not surprising. Luke Miller had always liked his women young and impressionable.

"How are you going to anchor this dam of yours?" Luke said, loud enough so that those behind him could hear the question, hear the challenge in his voice as well.

You would never guess he'd grown up in Gainesville, Florida, the son of a neurosurgeon and a University of Florida English professor. After a decade of living here, his accent was pure Southern Appalachian.

"A few small holes in the bedrock," Brennon said. "That's all we'll need. Nothing significant. Nothing anyone can see."

"To do that breaks federal law," Luke said. "It violates the Wild and Scenic Rivers Act of 1978."

Luke lifted a pair of wire-rimmed glasses from his shirt pocket. The glasses struck me as quite a concession for a man who prided himself on seeing things so clearly. The girl with the ponytail handed him some photocopied pages. I wondered if she and Luke lived together.

" 'It is hereby declared to be the policy of the United States that certain selected rivers of the Nation which, with their immediate environments, possess outstandingly remarkable scenic, recreational, geologic, fish and wildlife, historic, cultural, or other similar values, shall be preserved in free-flowing condition, and that they and their immediate environments shall be protected for the benefit and enjoyment of present and future generations.' "

Luke turned to another page. "To be even more specific," he said, " 'alteration or modification of the streambed will not be permitted.' "

He took off the glasses and looked not at Brennon but at Phillips.

"There it is in black and white. That's the law, and it's up to the Forest Service to enforce it."

Kowalsky came back to the podium to stand beside Brennon.

"That law is more ambiguous than you're making it appear," Kowalsky said. "That law didn't envision what's happened to my daughter."

"Let's take it to court then," Luke said. "That suits me fine."

"You'd like that, Miller, wouldn't you?" Kowalsky said, heat in his voice now. "Take a year or two to fight it out in court."

Brennon looked bewildered. "Are you telling me you

wouldn't want me to build this dam if it were your daughter?" he asked.

Luke handed the photocopies back to the girl. He took off his glasses and placed them back in his shirt pocket.

"I don't have a daughter," Luke said, his voice no longer confrontational, almost gentle. "But if I did and she was dead and I knew there was nothing I could do to make her alive again, I can't think of a place I'd rather her body be than in the Tamassee. I'd want her where she'd be part of something pure and good and unchanging, the closest thing to Eden we've got left. You tell me where there's a more serene and beautiful place on this planet. You tell me a more holy place, Mr. Brennon, because I don't know one."

Brennon hadn't expected that answer. He opened his mouth like he wanted to say something, but nothing came out. For a few moments no one else said anything either. It seemed as though we were all in abeyance, that Luke had taken us into that quiet, beautiful place where Ruth Kowalsky lay suspended. Luke sat down. The girl put her hand over his and kept it there.

He'd always been good with words, an English major before he quit college to come up here. Soon after Luke and I became lovers, he'd gone to Florida for six months. Occasionally he called, and twice that winter he drove up to Clemson to spend a weekend with me, but it had been his letters that made it so easy for me to fall in love despite the physical distance between us.

But this evening it wasn't just Luke's eloquence that made his words so powerful. Most people in the room knew he was voicing what he truly believed. He was voicing much of what I believed as well.

"That's a pretty place you've put Ruth," Kowalsky said, "and maybe it is a holy place." He looked at Luke as he spoke, and his words weren't sharp-edged with anger or irony. It was as though a truce had been called, a truce they both knew would soon enough be broken but which Kowalsky seemed to want to preserve a few moments longer. That was understandable, the need for a reprieve. Here was a man who had been able to get things done all his life through anger and intimidation and will, but also a man who'd now learned that none of what had made him a successful businessman could bring his daughter back. What could be worse for a man like that than to watch a river take your daughter under and not be able to do anything, to watch your wife dive into that river while you stood on the bank?

Then Kowalsky shook his head, and whatever vulnerability he'd allowed himself vanished so quickly it was almost as though it hadn't been there at all but something we had imagined for him.

"But my wife could never see it that way," he said. "No, our daughter can't be left in the river. I won't let that happen." He stepped back and turned to Brennon. "Go ahead and finish what you were saying."

"There's not much else to say, except this dam can be installed, used, and disassembled in one day. One day. One time." Brennon paused and looked around the room, then back at Kowalsky. He looked like he was trying to get his bearings. "I just don't understand why this is a problem," he said. He sounded not angry or even irritated, just bemused.

Luke stood up again. "It would set a precedent," he said. "It would open up the Tamassee for all sorts of damage. If you cut new trails for this you can cut them for ATVs. If you can put up a dam you can put up condominiums or a Ferris wheel and water slide and charge admission. What good is a law that's not enforced?"

Luke turned his gaze to Phillips.

"But that's not going to happen. The Forest Service's job is to enforce that law, a law the district ranger knows as well as anyone."

Kowalsky stepped closer to the podium again. "You've made your speech," he said to Luke. "Anybody else have anything to say or ask Mr. Brennon?"

"I got a question for you." Joel spoke from the side of the room. Like Randy and Ronny he wore a SEARCH AND RESCUE cap. Joel was tall and broad-shouldered like my father, and his jaw had the jut and set of that side of the family. His last name might be Lusk but he looked one-hundred-percent Glenn. He was like my father in other ways as well.

"You say you're from Illinois, right, Mr. Brennon?"

"That's right," Brennon said. "Carbondale."

"These portable dams of yours," Joel said, every syllable drawn out like taffy being stretched, "you've used them on rivers in Illinois?"

I didn't know where Joel was going with his questions, but he was doing it in classic southern good-old-boy fashion—as if he were dumb as a fence post. But he wasn't dumb, and whatever was on his mind was something he'd thought out or he wouldn't have spoken in the first place.

"That's right," Brennon said. "We've used them on a number of streams and rivers, not just in Illinois but Indiana as well."

"Flat slow-moving streams and rivers," Joel said, and it wasn't a question.

"Implying what?" Kowalsky said, taking a step from the podium, a step closer to Joel.

"I ain't implying nothing, I'm saying it," Joel said. "A white-water river's not like any other. Things that work on a flatland river won't work on the Tamassee."

"I think Mr. Brennon knows what his dam can do better than you," Kowalsky said.

"But he doesn't know this river," Joel said, "not the way those of us who've lived here all our lives know it."

It was obvious Kowalsky wasn't used to other people having the last word. His pupils seemed to contract. His glare swept across the room before settling again on Joel. Maybe he expected Joel to lower his eyes, but Joel stared back steadily, his eyes as implacable as Kowalsky's were intense, which only infuriated Kowalsky more. He let his glare shift slightly to include Ronny and Randy Moseley and several of the other men wearing SEARCH AND RESCUE caps. Luke's poetic imagery was forgotten now.

"Maybe you hillbillies don't know nearly as much about that river as you think," Kowalsky said. "I sure as hell haven't seen any indication you do."

If Kowalsky hadn't said *hillbillies*, Joel probably would not have replied the way he did. Things might have ended right there with Joel shrugging his shoulders or saying something like *we'll see*.

Joel spoke, his voice soft but loud enough. "We know enough not to let a twelve-year-old girl wade out in the middle of it during spring flooding."

"God damn you for saying that," Kowalsky shouted at Joel. Brennon grabbed Kowalsky's arm, holding him back.

That was enough for Walter Phillips. He joined Brennon and Kowalsky beside the lectern. "Let's try to keep this civil," he said, but we were way past that now. The room had grown as loud and animated as a tobacco auction. Groups formed near the front and in the aisles. Shouting among themselves, Luke and his river rats formed the largest, the most strident. Phillips stood behind the lectern and let people have at it a few minutes, maybe hoping that it would go out on its own, like a brush fire.

Joel turned and walked toward the door in slow, measured strides. He'd had his say and saw no further reason to hang around.

I looked at Allen. He leaned forward in his chair, his attention fixed on Kowalsky.

"Joel was out of line saying that," Billy said, "but I can hardly blame him, especially after that hillbilly crack. Kowalsky started badmouthing the Search and Rescue Squad soon as he got here. They've put up with a lot from that man."

Allen turned to Billy, his face incredulous.

"That man's lost his daughter," Allen said. "He just wants to get her out of the river, for God's sake."

Allen's outburst surprised me as much as it did Billy. In his book Allen had written about a massacre of Tutsis inside a Catholic church. In precise clinical detail he'd described the two hundred men, women, and children strewn around the altar. One phrase in particular had stuck in my mind: "a jigsaw puzzle of human limbs."

It was good to see him react emotionally, for as much as I had admired Allen's writing I'd found its unflinching gaze disconcerting. Reading his book had made me wonder, not for the first time in my life, if seeing too much suffering could overwhelm the heart. In my more generous moments I had wondered the same about Luke.

"PHILLIPS HAD BETTER WATCH OUT," BILLY SAID, AFTER SEVERAL minutes passed, "or this thing is going to get ugly real fast."

Sheriff Cantrell must have felt the same way, because he quickly stepped to the lectern and spoke to the ranger. Hubert McClure edged down the wall closer to Luke's group.

I searched the room for Earl Wilkinson. I was curious as to which side he was taking. He stood by himself near the back door. Although he hadn't been as instrumental as Luke, he'd done his share to get the Tamassee its Wild and Scenic status. But he was also a businessman. As Earl put more and more rafts on the river, some people, including Luke and Billy, had come to believe he was more interested in protecting his profit margin than the Tamassee.

Sheriff Cantrell stood conspicuously by the table as Walter Phillips stepped up to the podium.

"This meeting won't go on until people get back in their seats," Phillips shouted above the din. "Otherwise I'm adjourning it right now."

People lowered their voices and sat down.

"Does anyone who hasn't yet spoken have anything to say?" Phillips asked.

Harley Winchester stood up. He'd been sitting in the back row on the right side so his good eye faced the lectern. Harley wore steel-toed brogans and overalls. Sweat and dirt and grease stained his V-neck T-shirt.

"I got something to say."

Harley looked the room over, his dead right eye milky blue, unfocused. He'd lost that eye ten years ago while logging just outside the Tamassee's Wild and Scenic boundary. Someone had hammered a nail into a big oak, and Harley's chain saw hit it and sent a piece deep enough to plunge his right eye into darkness forever. Harley held Luke responsible for that nail being in the tree. Not that Luke had necessarily done it himself but that whoever did had been one of Luke's followers.

"I know how they done it twenty years ago," Harley said, his eye sweeping across the room. "They'd throw some dynamite in that pool and let the concussion free her. But things have changed on the river now, changed a lot. Twenty years ago I could cut timber anywhere on the Tamassee I wanted. I could cut a new logging road or float timber downstream if I needed. Now I can't log within a quarter mile of it. If I was to throw a rock in that river I'd probably get arrested."

Harley let his left eye settle on Luke.

"Of course it's different for rafting people and photographers. They can use that river to make money and then tell everybody else not to touch it, even to get a body out."

For a few seconds nobody said a word. Harley was in his fifties, but he could still outwork any of the other loggers. He carried a lot of weight in his belly now, but his arms were muscled like a pro football player's. He had a reputation for being strung tight as new barbed wire. People up here liked to stay on Harley's good side.

Luke did not bother to stand up.

"A camera or a raft accepts the river and its corridor as is, Harley. Nothing is altered."

"Touché," Billy said softly.

"Maybe we are worried a little too much about the river and not enough about people," said a man near the front I'd never seen before.

"Who's that?" I asked Billy.

"Tony Bryan."

"So that's Bryan."

"Yes," Billy said. "In the whole of his carpetbagging flesh."

I'd expected him to be older, at least in his fifties, not closer to forty. He was dressed in a green short-sleeved cotton shirt and khakis. What looked to be a Rolex glistened on his wrist.

"Well," said Billy. "Seems we've got all the major players present and accounted for."

Laurel Mist was Bryan's development. He'd built it two years ago and already sold all forty houses. According to the full-page ads I read each Sunday in *The Messenger*, he was ready to begin Phase Two, forty new homes bordering Licklog Creek, right up against the Tamassee's buffer zone.

"I agree with this man," Bryan said, nodding toward Harley. "Maybe the Tamassee should be allowed to serve all the people in this community."

Billy snorted. "Harley's exactly the kind of person Bryan built that guardhouse to keep out."

"Anybody can use that river who wants to," Luke said, standing up now and facing Bryan. "You can fish in it, float it, swim it, and picnic on its banks. You just don't have the right to destroy it."

"Who said anything about destroying it?" Bryan said. "You tree huggers never see beyond your own narrow focus. I've got just as much of an investment in keeping the Tamassee pristine as you do. That river's natural beauty is the best selling card I've got. Why would I hurt my own investment?"

The girl beside Luke stood up. "By the time the damage is evident, you'll have those lots and houses sold. And you know that, you bastard."

Bryan shook his head and smiled. "The greedy developer come to destroy Eden. That's the oldest cliché in the environmental-wacko handbook, isn't it."

"No," Luke said, "just the truest. Something only becomes a cliché when it happens repeatedly."

"Anything else?" Walter Phillips asked quickly, and you could tell he hoped hard there wasn't. "Then this meeting's adjourned."

I took my Nikon out of its case and shot Kowalsky as he said something to Phillips, then took a couple of shots of the crowd as they dispersed.

"I'm going up and talk to the father," Allen said, and moved through the crowd toward the front.

Luke and his entourage had left their seats and were heading for the door. I wondered if he'd seen me.

"Luke did pretty well," Billy said, standing up as well once the aisles cleared. "He was downright diplomatic, at least by his standards."

"Yes, he was," I said.

Allen shook hands with Kowalsky and Brennon at the podium while Myra Burrell sat at the table writing. Walter Phillips stood off to the side, watching the last of the crowd file out the door. The symbolism was perhaps a little too obvious, but as long as the caption wasn't something heavy-handed like *A man alone* or *Man in the middle* it could be a striking photograph. I raised my camera, focused on Phillips, and kept snapping until I'd used my remaining film.

Walter Phillips did not notice his picture being taken. He had appeared timid, even intimidated, during the meeting, but his profession tended to attract people more comfortable in solitude than in public. He was also new. I hoped that in these unguarded moments I might get one shot that revealed more about the man than had been discernible so far.

"I'm out of here," Billy said. "If you're still around tomorrow night, come by the store. Randall and Jeff are going to play. We'll get Margaret to sing."

In a few minutes everyone had left except for Allen, Brennon, Kowalsky, and Bryan, who had joined the other men up front. Phillips was waiting to lock up. There had been only three other reporters and one photographer in the room. Evidently the rest felt the real action was on the river itself.

I returned my camera to its case and walked outside. The air was cool, rinsed of the humidity of Columbia. The evening's first lightning bugs sent off their tiny flares as they hovered over weed tops. A bullfrog grunted in the creek that ran behind the community center as night settled into the valley like a slowly filling bath.

Luke had nearly drowned on a June evening like this one. Three days of rain had transformed the Tamassee into a brown torrent, but Luke wanted to run Bear Sluice in his kayak. We were on shore with several of the other river rats, all excellent kayakers themselves and not above taking a few risks. We'd been watching the river since midafternoon, waiting for it to clear and settle back into its banks. The others weren't about to go in and urged Luke to wait for morning as well. But Luke went in anyway and, as always, refused to wear a life jacket. Wearing one was cheating, he always said.

The hydraulic caught the kayak, sucked it in. A few moments later the kayak bobbed up like a cork, but Luke was still underwater. It seemed he was under an hour, but no more than three or four minutes passed before he emerged, neck and knees tucked to his chest as if shot out of a cannon.

He'd done what you are taught to do in such a situation—curl your body into a tight ball so the hydraulic spits you out. As Luke waded out of the water, his chest was heaving. He did not look frightened or even relieved.

"I thought you were going to drown," I had said, as we walked downstream to retrieve the kayak. I'd been trying to match Luke's composure, but my voice trembled as I spoke.

"I was fine," Luke said.

He had stopped walking and turned to me. The look on his face was more than just serene, it was beatific, like the faces of the raptured in Renaissance paintings. I thought he might be in shock.

"I didn't tuck until the last moment," Luke said. "Part of me wanted to stay. That hydraulic was like the still center of the universe."

The kayak had lodged on a sandbar. Luke had started to shiver, so I made him stay on shore while I waded out to it.

"It was like entering eternity," Luke had said as we'd made our way back up to Bear Sluice. "That's what the Celts believed—that water was a conduit to the next world. Maybe they were right."

Herb Kowalsky might not agree with what Luke had said about leaving the dead in the river, but Luke, unlike Kowalsky, had been to that place, and for Luke it had been beautiful.

JOEL'S TRUCK WAS STILL IN THE PARKING LOT, AND I WASN'T surprised when he called my name. He was behind the community center near the creek. The orange tip of his cigarette hovered before him as he stepped toward me.

"I didn't want to be in there no longer, but I didn't want to leave without speaking to you," Joel said.

"It's good to see you," I said, and gave him an awkward half hug.

"I probably shouldn't have spoken to that man the way I did," Joel said, "but he's been ragging on us ever since he got up here."

"That's what Billy said."

"You'd think losing a daughter to that river would make him understand how dangerous our job's been."

Joel took a final draw from his cigarette.

"When's Aunt Margaret getting back?" I asked.

"Tomorrow afternoon."

"So I'll see you both at Billy's tomorrow night?"

"We'll be there."

Joel threw down his cigarette and crushed it into the gravel with his boot heel.

"I best go," he said. "If I stay I'll just get in more trouble."

"I'll see you tomorrow night," I said.

Joel got in his truck and pulled out of the parking lot. For a few moments part of me followed that truck past Billy's store and down Damascus Church Road to a farmhouse I knew every bit as well as the one my father lived in. "Come on home with me," Aunt Margaret would say every other Friday night. "I'm tired of dealing with four boys. I need me a sweet little girl to spoil." The house she and my Uncle Mark lived in had a tin roof, and the nights it rained were always the best. After Ben and I had gotten burned, I slept there often, leaving my own bed and walking the quarter mile to Aunt Margaret's house wearing pajamas, a coat, and shoes. I always slept deep and peaceful under that tin roof.

CHAPTER 4

You're a wanderer, Aunt Margaret had told me. *It's the way you look at the mountains; you want to know what's on the other side. And you'll never come near being content till you do know.* I was eight years old and we were picking blackberries on the east slope of Sassafras Mountain. We had come early, dew soaking our shoes as we sidled up land slanted as a barn roof, shiny milk pails in our hands. Morning sun brightened the mountainside as our first berries pinged the metal. Black-and-yellow writing spiders had cast their webs between some of the bushes, and dew beads twinkled across them like strung diamonds. My fingers purpled as my pail began slowly to fill, a soft, cushiony sound as berry fell on berry. The sun sipped away the last dew from the webs, and I started to sweat under Uncle Mark's long-sleeved flannel shirt. My arm ached from the pail's weight. The thin handle dug its imprint on my palm. I sat down in a gap among the bushes, my gaze crossing over Tamassee toward Licklog Mountain. Aunt Margaret had come and stood behind me, her hand brushing leaf litter from my hair as she spoke.

Aunt Margaret's prophecy had been correct, for college and each new job took me farther from the mountains—first Clemson, then Laurens, and now Columbia. It had not been until the Columbia move that I recognized a steady eastward migration toward Charleston, toward a place I could look out my office window and see not mountains but the Atlantic Ocean.

But I was back now, at least for a little while, traveling the same road as that morning we'd returned from Sassafras Mountain, Aunt Margaret driving as I kept the pails full of blackberries from spilling.

I glanced at Allen and knew he was already working, mapping a lead paragraph for his article or a possible follow-up question for Brennon or Phillips.

"They're going to meet at Wolf Cliff Falls tomorrow at eleven," he said, as we pulled into the motel parking lot. He got out and I slid behind the wheel. After closing the door, he leaned in the window.

"Brennon is going to look over the area where he wants the dam. Phillips and Kowalsky will be there too, so I'll have a chance to talk with all of them more in-depth. Maybe you can get some good photos as well."

"I probably can," I said.

"Kowalsky said I could ride out with them, but I said you'd know how to get there."

"I'll come by at nine," I said.

"Good. I'll be waiting in the lobby."

Allen stepped away but I spoke anyway.

"Sounds like Kowalsky is going out of his way to make your job easy."

"So far at least."

"Is he a fan of your work?"

"Not that I know of. He said Hudson contacted him, told him I'd be covering the story." Allen paused. "Hudson told him I'd be more understanding than other reporters because of what had happened to my wife and daughter."

He turned away before I could respond. Glancing back, he raised his hand, then walked toward his room.

I pulled out of the lot, drove past Billy's store, and took a right onto Damascus Church Road. The few houses I passed, including Aunt Margaret's, were dark. The road curved a last time and I turned right at the battered mailbox with GLENN hand-painted on its side. Gravel crunched and spun under the wheels as I drove up to the house. No porch light lit the steps, and the moon was waning. But the stars were out, so much brighter than in Columbia. They looked closer up here as well, as though each one had been picked up and polished, then set nearer to the earth.

I knocked and no light came on, so I knocked harder, hard enough that my knuckles stung. Finally the front bedroom light came on. I heard movement toward the door, then the sound of a latch unfastening.

Daddy stepped back to let me come in. He wore a green pair of pajamas that probably hadn't been washed in weeks. His eyes were dulled and unfocused. They registered no surprise, though I hadn't told him I was coming.

"How long you been knocking?"

I set the suitcase beside the fireplace. "A little while."

"That medicine the doctors gave me puts me under pretty good. If I'd been in the back bedroom I'd yet be sleeping."

He rubbed his eyes with his knuckles, the way a drowsy child might.

"You go on back to bed," I said. "I know where everything is."

"I can make us some coffee," he said. "That'll wake me up."

"There's no need to do that. Soon as I unpack I'm going to bed myself."

I hoped the medicine would make him too groggy to argue. That way I'd at least get a night's sleep before we started in on each other. I bent to pick up the suitcase and carry it on into the back bedroom.

"Seldom as you come," he said, "it don't seem fitting to speak no more than a half-dozen words and then be off to bed."

"It's late, Daddy. I'm tired from the trip up here. You're tired. We can talk tomorrow."

"All right," he said, the petulance draining from his voice. "I'll make that coffee in the morning."

We stood there looking at each other a few moments, keeping our distance. We hadn't kissed or hugged and I knew we wouldn't. I remembered how he'd pulled up a chair beside

Momma's bed those last days. He'd sit there for six hours without once getting up but never hold her hand or kiss her forehead. "He carries what he feels for people deep inside. Even as a kid he was that way," Aunt Margaret said. "Your momma knows that." But I had wondered then as I did now what good love was that couldn't be expressed.

"Good night," I said.

I walked through the kitchen, toward the back bedroom, past Ben's room. I knew if I paused and turned on the light the room would be much as it had been fifteen years ago: paperbacks and fishing magazines filling a bookshelf, a couple of rods propped up in a corner, chest of drawers. No mirror.

I WOKE TO MEMORY—THE YELLOW-FLOWERED WALLPAPER I hung in the ninth grade, the poster I bought at a Ricky Scaggs concert, the bureau mirror where Momma and I checked my dress the evening of my senior prom. And the bed where I lay, the same bed my mother had died in my junior year at Clemson.

That spring, pill bottles had lined the bureau, and a bedpan lay under the night table. The indentation of my mother's body and head remained on the mattress and pillow each time we lifted her up. The room seemed dark even when the curtains had been pulled all the way back, and no matter the number of times Aunt Margaret and I opened the windows or cleaned the room it always seemed dank and musty like a root cellar.

Those weekends I slept on the couch. Ben, who drove the truck down to Clemson to pick me up on Fridays, took me back to school Sunday evenings. My grades suffered that semester, and I almost lost my scholarship.

On those Saturdays I stayed with Momma while Daddy and Ben planted the spring crops. Though she never said it outright, Momma made it clear she expected me to set things right between Daddy and Ben and me, that this burden was mine and mine alone now. What I wanted to say was *Why is it me who has to forgive? How can you expect me to do what you couldn't?* But how could I say such things when she lay there dying?

When I wasn't tending Momma I cleaned the house and made lunch and supper. Sundays after church Aunt Margaret sent Joel over with yellowware filled with fried chicken and snap beans and rice. By then Momma was too weak to sit with us at the table. Daddy would say a short prayer, and that was more words than were said the rest of the meal.

Now my father was dying in the same house.

I made my way to the kitchen. More memories—my mother making fruitcakes at Christmas, my clumsy attempts to cook for her and Daddy and Ben, the *Farmer's Almanac* calendar that predicted snow months in advance. And of course what I always thought about when I entered this room: the pot of pole beans on the stove, my brother's hand reaching for the handle.

The smell of the coffee did not rouse Daddy, so I poured myself a cup and went back to the bedroom. I set up my laptop on the bed and plugged it into the phone jack. I typed in Allen's name and pulled up about forty thousand listings, then narrowed the search. A number were passing references, others reprints of articles he'd written, but I found several interviews and a *Newsweek* profile. Pieces that revealed, among other things, that Allen had had extensive assignments in Belfast, Kosovo, and Cambodia as well as Rwanda.

My eye was drawn to a comment he made in an interview in the *Atlanta Journal-Constitution*. The subject at hand was the limitations of photography. "There is always more that lies outside the camera's framed mechanical truth," he'd said. "A photograph is voiceless. Neither its subject nor its producer can explain the suffering or injustice, give it a context. It's up to a man or woman using the human tool of language to do that."

It was an eloquent statement but also rather grandiose, and I wasn't convinced.

I kept searching for what I was really after, not stopping until Claire Pritchard-Hemphill's face appeared on the screen. I scanned the article's caption and understood not only why Kowalsky would cooperate with Allen but also why Allen still wore his wedding band.

Claire Pritchard-Hemphill wore her hair longer than most thirty-four-year-old mothers, the dark hair cascading down her shoulders. No mommy cut for this woman. She looked sure of herself, the type who could do the wife and mother thing and still put on a dark skirt and jacket and hold her own in a boardroom. The lips were thick and sensual, the eyes dark as her hair. She smiled slightly in the photograph, a private smile created as much with her eyes as her lips. EDUCATOR, DAUGHTER KILLED IN CAR WRECK, the caption beneath the photograph read.

Claire Pritchard-Hemphill, thirty-four, died Friday afternoon
at Georgetown University Hospital. Ms. Pritchard-Hemphill
taught political science at Northern Virginia Community College. A daughter, Miranda Kay Hemphill, nine, also died in
the accident which occurred on the George Washington Parkway at 2:40 P.M. Friday. No other cars were involved. Police
say a heavy rainstorm was a contributing factor. She was the
wife of *Washington Post* journalist Allen Hemphill.

I entered Claire Pritchard-Hemphill's name into the search
engine and pulled up another obituary. Born in Landover,
Maryland, BA and MA earned at the University of Maryland,
both parents and a sister surviving her as well as a husband.
A different picture headed this piece, a more informal one
with Miranda, their faces pressed close together as they
smiled at the camera. The child had her mother's dark hair
but her father's features. She looked happy and confident.
From the way she leaned into her mother you knew she was
an affectionate child, a child who would crawl into bed with
her parents on weekend mornings, a child who would give
hugs and kisses before going to school. I wondered if Allen
had taken this photograph, had been the person they smiled
for.

I was staring at the picture when Daddy tapped on
the door.

"I thought I heard you up and about," he said.

He wore patched corduroy pants that sagged low on his
bony hips and a V-neck T-shirt, white hairs tufting from his

sunken chest. The doctor had told Ben that Daddy had lost fifty pounds.

"I got cereal in the pantry," Daddy said. "That's about all the breakfast I can eat anymore. If I'd of known you was coming I'd have bought some eggs and bacon."

He stepped into the room and stood next to the bed.

"Cereal is fine," I said, and exited the screen.

"You should have let me know you was coming, Maggie."

"I didn't know I was coming myself till the last minute," I said, trying not to sound irritated, trying and failing. Here we go again, I thought, always able to find some way to rub each other wrong. "I've already made coffee," I said, picking up my cup and stepping past him. "I'll get you a cup."

Daddy sat down at the table as I poured his coffee and refilled my cup. I placed my fingers around the handles and lifted the sugar bowl off the counter as well.

"You're going to burn yourself," Daddy said.

I glanced at him sharply as I set down the sugar bowl and cup, took a seat at the other end of the table. Between us lay wooden salt and pepper shakers Aunt Margaret had given Momma, a napkin holder Ben mitered in shop class placed beside them.

"I see you got yourself a new car."

"No sir," I said, "that's the newspaper's car. I helped cover the meeting about the drowned girl last night."

Daddy stirred sugar into his coffee and took a tentative sip before adding another spoonful. "They get much of anything settled at that meeting?"

"They spent most of the time getting each other riled up."

"What they ought to do is what they done in the old days," Daddy said. "Throw a stick of dynamite in there and be done with it."

"That's what Harley Winchester said."

"Well, it works, and I'll bet better than any harebrained scheme of building a temporary dam." Daddy shook his head. "There's always somebody coming up here to tell us how to do things, everything from what trees we can cut to whether a man can put a trailer on his own land. They never seem to realize we'd been doing just fine before they showed up with all their advice."

Daddy waited for me to respond. When I didn't he took another sip of coffee, then looked out the window to where the milk cow waited outside the barn.

"Joel's running late today and that cow don't like it a bit." Daddy continued looking out the window as he spoke. "I reckon he was at the meeting."

"Yes sir, but I doubt he'll be at another. Joel and the girl's father got into it."

"I'm not much surprised. That fellow's been riding him and the twins pretty hard, saying they're not doing enough when it's them in there risking their lives while he's up on the bank. Did you hear what happened to Randy?"

"No sir."

"He was using an underwater camera and he got too close to the hydraulic. It tore the mask right off his face. He was lucky that's all it got."

Daddy looked out the window again. He'd always taken a

lot of pride in the way his farm looked, crop rows so straight you'd have thought they'd been marked off with a plumb line, hay bales stacked in the barn loft with the precision of a mason laying brick. What he saw now was a barbed-wire fence that needed mending, a barn roof browned by rust, a pulp-wood truck whose tires were flat from dry rot. Nothing sprouted but broom sedge in the bottomland, and the pond held more silt than water. He was dying and his farm was dying with him.

He scratched the white hairs sprouting on his chin. Just as he'd kept everything on his farm tidy, he'd done the same with his own appearance. He'd shaved every morning, and when he came in from his fields he never sat down at the supper table without taking a shower first. But that didn't seem very important to him now. Maybe letting things go made it easier.

Daddy took another sip of coffee, a longer sip. Coffee dribbled onto his chin like tobacco juice.

"Can't run a farm, can't hardly even swallow no more," he said. He wiped his chin with the back of his hand. "If it wasn't for that chemotherapy I might be able to do more things. That stuff's probably killing me more than the cancer."

"I could milk her. I haven't forgot how."

"No, Joel will be here directly. He just has to get his own chores done first."

Daddy looked at the salt shakers. "I reckon Luke Miller was there last night."

"Yes."

"And talking all his nonsense."

"He had his say."

Daddy looked at me. I knew he wanted to comment more and probably would, not just about Luke but about Luke and me.

"Let's not talk about Luke now," I said.

My father's hands lay on the table before him and they trembled.

"I got things I need to say," he said.

I had never seen him cry, not when he'd visited Ben in the hospital, not when Momma died. But he looked as though he might do so now. It's the medicine, I told myself.

"I don't want to talk about it," I said, and finished my coffee with one long swallow. I could always eat breakfast at Mama Tilson's.

I stood up and pushed the chair back under the table and went to the bedroom. I locked the door behind me and shoved clothes and toiletries into my suitcase.

It wasn't my first quick exit from this house. I'd been work-ing with Luke a month when I asked to stay overnight. We were in chairs we'd brought out to the cabin's porch, not so much sitting as sprawling, our bodies, especially arms, suc-cumbing to gravity after a day muscling rapids and sluices. A minute passed before Luke spoke.

"You sure you want to do that?" he asked.

"Why wouldn't I be?"

"Because you're going to hurt your father bad, and he's already had a hard enough year with your mother dying."

Luke's words surprised me.

"You're not scared of him, are you?" I asked.

"No," Luke said, "but this is going to change things between you two."

I laughed. "Well, maybe then it will help, because it can't get any worse. If something changes between us, it can only be for the better."

My birthday had been two days earlier, and I reminded Luke of this fact.

"I'm twenty-one," I said. "I make my own choices now."

So that night Luke did not drive me down Damascus Church Road to my father's house. I did not sleep well, perhaps because I wasn't used to sharing a bed, perhaps because my resolve was weakening. I finally got up and checked Luke's watch. Three A.M. It wasn't too late. I could wake Luke and have him drive me home. Daddy would have some words for me about coming in so late, but I would be there before daybreak, and that would make all the difference. To him it would be a sign of deference, an acknowledgment of where my home was.

But I hadn't done that. Instead, I turned on the lamp and read until my eyes blurred. Only then did I sleep. When I woke, light streaked through the cabin's back window and someone was knocking on the front door.

"It's my father," I told Luke.

Luke sat on the side of the bed and reached for a pair of shorts and a T-shirt.

I grabbed his forearm. "Go on and answer the door."

Luke stared at me, waiting for some explanation.

"Don't put your clothes on."

"I'm not doing that," Luke said, jerking his arm free. He

put on the shorts and shirt, then walked across the gray, rough boards and opened the door. Daddy stared at Luke, then past him to where I lay in the bed.

"I've packed up your things and they're on the front porch," he said. The words were spoken softly, which was more unsettling than the anger and self-righteousness I'd expected.

Then Daddy looked at Luke, his voice still low but the inflection sharp as a scythe blade.

"If I thought it to make any matter of difference, I'd beat the hell out of your worthless ass."

I did not sleep in my father's house again until Christmas, when Ben begged Daddy into letting me come back, begged me to be willing. But I stayed only two nights, and my visits ever since had been even briefer.

I WALKED INTO THE FRONT ROOM. DADDY STOOD BY THE front door. He had weighed over two hundred pounds most of his life, but now he wouldn't have pushed a bathroom scale's needle past one-fifty. His clothes hung as loose on him as they would on a scarecrow.

"I've got to go," I said and tried to brush past him. His hand reached out and held my arm. There was still enough strength left in that hand to hold me for a few moments.

"The first night after I heard that girl had drowned I dreamed about it," Daddy said. "I dreamed I was looking down in the water and her face was looking right back at me. The water was clear and still, and I could feature every part of her face like it was a picture under glass."

I jerked out of his grasp, my suitcase bumping his leg as I passed. My back was to him as he finished speaking.

"Only it wasn't that girl's face in the water, Maggie. It was yours."

WOLF CLIFF IS A PLACE WHERE NATURE HAS GONE OUT OF ITS way to make humans feel insignificant. The cliff itself is two hundred feet of granite that looms over the gorge. A fissure jags down its gray face like a piece of black embedded lightning. The river tightens and deepens. Even water that looks calm moves quick and dangerous. Mid-river fifty yards above the falls, a beech tree thick as a telephone pole balances like a footbridge on two haystack-tall boulders. A spring flood set it there twelve years ago.

The falls itself flows between two boulders only eight feet apart and spills into a pool big and deep enough to cover a house trailer. The boulder on the left side of the falls leans into the pool. A good rock to dive off, except that here countercurrent forms a hydraulic and, behind that hydraulic, a deep undercut, an undercut where Ruth Kowalsky's body was suspended between earth and sky.

Twenty feet upstream, Ronny and Randy measured water depth and searched for bedrock to anchor Brennon's polyurethane dam. They worked alone except for the people onshore, who held the ropes knotted around the brothers' waists. Joel and the other members of Tamassee Search and Rescue had refused to help. Some local people sat on rocks below the falls, but they soon got bored and left.

Brennon, Kowalsky, and Phillips stood together on the shore, Brennon and Kowalsky holding the ropes out in front of them as if fishing. A woman from the *Oconee Tribune* was with them, a *Greenville News* reporter standing a few yards away waiting his turn. On the opposite bank an *Atlanta Journal-Constitution* reporter and photographer stood forlorn as castaways. They'd come in on the Georgia side. The reporter was thirty yards away from the people he needed to talk to, but it might just as well have been a mile. He'd tried shouting a few questions to Phillips, but the white water rendered his words unintelligible. He finally gave up and studied a Forest Service map.

The photographer stepped to the river edge and began shooting. Like more and more photographers, especially at the bigger papers, he had made the switch to a digital camera. Lee had been pressing me to convert as well, to learn Photoshop software. He'd used my resistance as another opportunity to joke about my Appalachian backwardness and nostalgia for the good old days of outhouses and oil lamps.

But my resistance was aesthetic. When I took a shot I didn't want high-tech silence. I wanted the mechanical click, the way it signaled like a trap being sprung that something was captured. I wanted the process to be visceral.

"I'd rather talk to those guys without anyone else around," Allen said, "but I guess I'll go over and listen in."

"I'm going to sit down," I said.

"I'll join you in a little while," Allen said.

I walked twenty yards below the falls and found a long chunk of driftwood the river had tossed on the bank. I sat down and closed my eyes. The air quality was as poor now in the mountains as anywhere in the state, the scientists claimed, and all the proof your own eyes needed was to look at the higher mountaintops and see the brown-needled spruce and fir trees. The same acid rain that killed those cedars fell into the Tamassee, but as I took a deep breath it was hard to believe there could be any place purer in the world.

During my childhood, even after she'd gotten a washing machine, Aunt Margaret carried her quilts each spring to the river. Knee deep in the flow, she let hands, lye soap, and water rub away winter's grime, give the quilts a fresh, bright smell you couldn't get any other way. Nights she had tucked me under those quilts I'd listened for what she claimed I'd hear if I were quiet enough—the sound of the water still flowing through the cloth.

I opened my eyes and looked twenty yards upstream where Ruth Kowalsky's body lay under a pall of white water. Farther upstream, Allen talked to the *Greenville News* reporter. He raised his hand and pointed to the falls, and the gold wedding band caught the morning sun.

I returned my gaze to the pool that held Ruth Kowalsky's body. What would Allen, who'd lost his own child, feel in this gorge? It could only be painful, like stitches on a half-healed wound being ripped open.

I hadn't said much on the drive from the motel. Allen was subdued as well, no doubt preparing for what he'd be confronting. When he asked how the visit with my father had been, I'd said something about it being the same as always and we'd left it at that.

We had been the first to arrive. As we'd walked into the
gorge, the last remnants of morning fog coiled around our feet.
Mushrooms lined the trail, including some Death's Caps. The
sun hadn't risen over Wolf Cliff yet, and the canopy of oak
and hickory made the light wan and splotchy—like the
haunted wood of a sinister fairy tale, I'd thought, as we'd
made our way to where a dead girl waited.

AT TEN-THIRTY, LUKE AND THE BLOND GIRL CAME INTO VIEW
upstream. They beached their canoe on the Georgia side
twenty yards above where Ronny and Randy worked. Luke
and the girl sat on the bank. They didn't talk much. They had
come to guard the river.

After a while the county reporter tucked her note pad into
the back pocket of her jeans and headed up the trail, leaving
the *Greenville News* reporter alone with Phillips and Kowalsky. Brennon stood away from them, pencil and spiral notebook in hand. All the while Ronny and Randy continued to
wade upstream and down, one side to the other. They waded
slowly, heads down, eyes inches from the surface as they
stabbed measuring sticks into the water like spears.

They shouted depths and bedrock placements to Brennon,
who recorded them. I took some photos of Ronny and Randy
working and then some of the falls.

"Quite a scene," Allen said, coming over to stand beside me.

"Yes," I said. "And nothing's even happened yet, at least
officially."

Allen nodded toward the Greenville reporter.

"That guy says his paper is putting this on the front page. They're even doing a poll about whether or not to allow the dam."

"That seems like a bit much."

"I thought so too."

The *Greenville News* reporter left. Allen walked upstream to join Brennon and Kowalsky, while I returned to the piece of driftwood and sat down. A yellow butterfly settled for a few moments on a nearby rock, its wings opening and closing like slow applause. Gnats hovered around my face. The sun was directly overhead now, shining down as if into a well. The shallows sparkled with mica, probably some gold as well. There had been a time when locals panned the Tamassee, but that was illegal now given its Wild and Scenic status. A buzzard circled overhead, not a turkey buzzard but a smaller black one. Luke had once told me they could smell something dead from a distance of six miles.

Like Allen, I had questions I wanted to ask, but they were for him, not for Brennon or Kowalsky or Phillips. This wasn't the place, though. Death was too close here. It surfaced out of the ground and lingered in the sky and in the water.

I wondered if Lee had known about Allen's family and, if so, why he hadn't bothered to tell me. Even if Lee hadn't known, Hudson did. Hudson had never impressed me as an especially sensitive man, but sending a reporter who'd lost his own daughter to cover this story seemed more than merely insensitive. It seemed cruel.

I made a final swat at the gnats, then hiked back up a trail that had widened significantly in the past week. Fifty yards up I veered right into a stand of blackjack oaks. Soon granite outcrops replaced trees and dirt. I stepped carefully among the boulders, perfect places for timber rattlesnakes to sun. In a few minutes the left face of Wolf Cliff loomed directly above me, and I stood in front of a cave Ben and I had found two decades earlier.

We had not gone inside the day we discovered it. The entrance was well concealed and narrow. Ben and I wanted to see if the cave got bigger before we risked squeezing feet first through the mouth. We came back the following afternoon, the flashlight we sneaked out of the house jammed in the back pocket of my cut-off jeans. We left our bikes at the bridge and walked down the river trail toward Wolf Cliff.

I went in first and was able to stand after a few yards. I helped Ben inside, then aimed the flashlight's beam in front of my feet the same way a blind person might use a cane. The cave was cool and moist like a springhouse. Glossy black salamanders wiggled away from the light, and somewhere water dripped. We kept going until the cave widened a last time, became the size of a room. In the center a mound of ashes smeared the cave floor black.

"Someone camped here," I told Ben. "But why in the back of a musty old cave?"

"So they wouldn't be seen," Ben said.

I swept the light across the campsite, then onto the cave walls.

"What is it?" Ben asked.

I moved the light slowly across an image of a human being, a crude stick figure, arms upraised.

"Maybe the Cherokees left it," I told Ben. "Some kind of sign."

"But what does it mean?"

I studied the figure more closely, particularly the blank face that, like the arms, was raised upward.

"I think someone was hurting and this is the way they prayed for help."

"Yes," Ben said, and reached out to touch the figure with his index finger.

Knowing that long ago other people had been here, people now dead for centuries, made me uneasy. I never returned to the cave, but Ben did many times that summer. When it was suppertime I would walk down the trail, then scramble up to the cave entrance. I'd call and he would soon emerge, shielding his eyes as he stepped back into the light.

I stepped away from the same opening now and headed back to the river, to my spot on the log. Allen was still talking with Phillips and Kowalsky, their words unintelligible. Luke and the girl sat on the other bank, but Luke was no longer looking at Ronny and Randy. He looked right at me.

He had stripped down to a pair of blue nylon river shorts. He carried more weight around his midsection now, but his arms and upper legs were still visibly muscled from paddling and hiking. Luke said something to the girl before walking downstream. He descended the riverbank stiffly, then swam across, lifting himself onto the stone slab. I recognized the mole on his right breast, the long purple scar just below it where a submerged tree branch had gashed him. Another whiter, less visible, scar marked where a river rock had cracked three ribs.

"Still on our side?" Luke asked. His scarred knees, an intersection of stitch tracks from the various cartilage and ligament tears, popped as he sat down beside me. He winced, flexed his right knee several times as if it were a gate hinge that wouldn't close properly.

"I didn't know photographers took sides. Cameras record reality."

Luke wiped water off his face with the back of his hand. "I taught you better than that, Maggie. You know there is always more than one reality."

Luke's eyes had been the first thing I'd noticed about him when we'd met. Somewhere between green and blue. The color of the Tamassee's deepest pools on sunny days—if viewed from a ridge trail. When you were actually on the river you didn't see that color. You saw through the pool to the rocks and sand at the bottom. Luke's eyes were like that. When you looked into them it seemed you saw not into but through them, toward a place of utter clarity.

"So tell me the realities, Luke," I said, looking away.

"A father who's lost his daughter to a river and can't accept it. A businessman getting free national advertising for his product. A developer using this incident to weaken environmental regulations."

Up close, I was surprised at how much older he seemed, not just the lines on his face and thinning hair but also his voice. It was as if the river had worn him down the way it might a rock or bank.

"So what's your reality, Luke?" I asked.

"The river. That's the reality that matters. It's natural law and, I might add, federal law as well."

"There was a time you weren't quite so enamored of federal law, a time when you didn't have any problem breaking laws, federal or otherwise, to block a logging road or grow a few pot plants."

"The law's on the right side now."

Ronny and Randy waded out of the river. They unknotted the ropes from their waists as they talked to Brennon.

"So Allen Hemphill's covering this?"

"Yes. He'll probably want to talk to you."

"Sure, I'll give him the party line, but it won't do any good. He'll get his story from Kowalsky. That's the only one he's interested in."

"Why do you think that?"

"Because I've read his book. Those blurbs on the back, 'Allen Hemphill is a journalist who casts a cold eye on life, on death,' blah, blah, blah—that's utter bullshit. He's a sentimentalist. By the time most people finish his book, Hemphill's manipulated them into weeping and gnashing their teeth."

"How do you expect people not to be outraged by the massacre of children?"

"A good photographer should know the answer to that question."

"Enlighten me, Luke."

"You use a wider lens. You show what would have happened had these children not been massacred. You ask what's really crueler, being hacked to death in a few seconds or dying from starvation or AIDS."

"Maybe that can be changed as well."

"It would be nice to believe that, but human history argues otherwise."

Luke fixed his eyes on mine, and this time I did not avoid his gaze.

"You getting sentimental on me? Or are you just a little sweet on Hemphill? I see the way you lean in to catch his words, the way you keep glancing upstream to make sure he's still there. You can't fool me. I know you too well."

"Maybe I'm not the same person I was eight years ago."

"I think you are," Luke said. "You just conceal it better now."

I looked across the river at Luke's companion. At her age I would have had my eye on Luke if he were talking to another woman, but she was lying on her stomach reading a book. "To answer your question, maybe it's just that I'm capable of some basic human emotions."

"What basic human emotions are you talking about? Greed, hate, fear? Those tend to predominate, from what I've seen of the world."

"There are others. Just because you don't possess them doesn't mean another person can't."

Luke stood up, ran his fingers through his hair. "Like love," he said. "That's what you're saying, right?"

"Maybe so."

"I know more about love than you do," he said, looking not at the blond but at the Tamassee.

"A river's not human, Luke."

"No, it's something better. A human being's puny compared to a river." He raised his eyes from the river. "And maybe that's the purest kind of love, Maggie, because I don't expect the river to love me back. There was a time you knew these things." His voice softened. "Maybe you've forgotten I did an extended tour of duty in the lovers-of-mankind brigade. And that I did it on the front lines."

"I haven't forgotten," I said.

At night or when a hard rain made the river too high to run, we used to stay in the cabin and read. Luke had nailed four bookshelves together, and the shelves and the books they held covered the back wall. Luke claimed he could educate me better than a university could. And maybe he did, because the books I read affected me in a way assigned texts in college never had.

My family had lived in Oconee County for over two hundred years. Seven generations of Glenn eyes had opened and closed in this place, but it took writers such as William Bartram and Horace Kephart, men from other parts of the country, to reveal what had surrounded me all my life. Luke tutored me on the river as well, explaining not just about eddy lines and hydraulics but also the watershed's plant and wildlife. He taught me how mountain laurel leaves were glossy and rhododendron weren't, how on mink tracks you could see the claws where on otters you saw only the pads.

And he read me poetry written and set in distant places, as though I had first to see another world to see my own. That very thing happening when Wordsworth wrote of a mountain spring's "soft inland murmur" or Hopkins described "rose-moles all in stipple upon trout that swim." In my literature classes at Clemson I had enjoyed poetry, but it had seemed exotic. Luke brought it into the world I knew.

And after Bartram and Kephart and the poets, he had me read Edward Abbey and Wendell Berry and Peter Matthiessen to learn how ephemeral a wild place could be.

He told me about Biafra as well.

Their eyes were the only thing that remained alive and human, Luke said. Lifting them had been like lifting kites, because that was what their bodies had become, stick bones with papery flesh glued to them.

After a week in the aid camp, Luke believed the situation was hopeless. The victorious FMG had herded three million Ibo refugees into a region of only 2,500 square kilometers, an area the war had turned into a wasteland of destroyed homes, markets, and hospitals. A few of the ravaged had risen from their cots and gone home, but too often they returned. Most died within twenty-four hours of their arrival. There was never a shortage of replacements to fill the cots.

Luke's assignment there had been for six months but he'd stayed eighteen.

"Long enough to earn my lifelong furlough from any other obligations to humanity," he'd told me one night when a bottle of wine made him more talkative than usual. "The day I flew out of Owerri, I looked out the plane window and watched it disappear. Free to love or not love, care or not care. Free to find one good, pure thing in the world and save that thing. That's all you can do anyway."

He was saying the same thing now. I looked across the river at a girl only slightly older than I'd been when I'd read Luke's books, slept in his bed.

"I'm sorry I've disappointed you," I said. "Maybe you'll have better luck with her."

"Maybe I will. Carolyn was majoring in chemical engineering when I met her, gearing up to spend the next thirty years as a lackey for Dow Chemical. Now she's studying environmental law."

"So you've saved her soul."

Luke did not smile. "Those are her words, not mine."

"What's her reading assignment today?"

"Matthiessen's *Wildlife in America*," Luke said. "One of your favorites, as I recall."

"So when can Allen talk to you?"

"Six o'clock at Mama Tilson's. Grassroots environmentalists don't have expense accounts, so tell him he's paying. We'll eat and then talk. You be there too. Sounds like you need some review on what's at stake."

He looked over at Ronny and Randy, who had put on their T-shirts and boots.

"Looks like they're through for today, so I guess I'll go on."

Brennon pointed out something on the far shore to Phillips

while Allen and Kowalsky talked. Ronny and Randy waved, then disappeared up the trail to their truck.

"I don't know why those guys are helping Kowalsky," Luke said, "especially after last night."

"Because they're decent men trying to do some good. They have children. It's called empathy, another basic human emotion."

"Is that it?" Luke said. "I thought they were so thick-headed they didn't know when they'd been insulted." He smiled. "See you at supper, Maggie."

Luke dove into the river and swam back across. He and Carolyn got into the canoe and drifted beneath Wolf Cliff into the slow water that ended a half mile downstream at Five Falls.

YOU'RE GOING TO HURT YOUR FATHER BAD, LUKE HAD SAID. AND that was what I had wanted. Because being connected to Daddy was like having an infected limb no antibiotic could cure. What I wanted was not only to sever the limb but also to cauterize it.

I learned a lot from Luke that summer. He taught me to sight on the surface what lay beneath water—the snags and undercuts. He showed me the Tamassee was not one river but many, depending on the time of year, the amount of rain, the amount of visibility.

He taught me how to use a camera as well, how to manipulate shutter speed and light, how balance and perspective were as important in photography as painting. He never used color film, despite frequent complaints from the rafting company's clients. Luke believed you saw the essentials in black and white, that color was nothing more than decoration and distraction.

He was a good teacher. The following spring when I graduated with my English degree, I'd taken a job with the Clemson town newspaper. I wrote articles, but photography was what I did best, winning some state awards for weeklies. When the Laurens paper called, they were looking for a photographer, not a writer.

Now I watched as Luke and Carolyn grew smaller, the downstream angle such that they appeared cut in half, their heads, arms, and torsos bobbing in the current.

I wondered if Carolyn possessed the cool cynicism so many women her age displayed toward relationships. The way she'd reached for Luke's hand at the meeting seemed to argue otherwise. That was something I would have done, had done.

I remembered the early August night Luke spent not with me but at the Tamassee Motel with Janice, the woman he'd stayed with in Florida.

"I thought it was just you and me," I told Luke the next morning after she left. I'd spent a tearful, sleepless night on the cabin's couch, listening for Luke's pickup to turn into the makeshift driveway.

"Have I ever told you that?" Luke said. He touched my chin with his finger and raised my eyes to his. "Have I ever asked you not to be with anyone else?"

"No," I said. "I just believed we were together and for a long time."

"I've been honest with you," Luke said. "More honest than you've been with me." He removed his finger from my chin. "I think a lot of what I am to you is a way to get back at your father."

"That's a lie. I couldn't have done the things we've done," I said. "I love you." Those three syllables felt strange on my tongue, because I couldn't remember saying them even as a child. Not even to my mother as she lay in my bed dying.

Luke said nothing.

"But you don't love me. Do you love her?"

"No," Luke said.

I turned to start packing, but Luke pulled me back and kissed me on the mouth. When I didn't respond, he touched my cheek with his fingers.

"She's gone back to Florida, Maggie," he said. "You and I have had a good summer together, and we still have some time before you go back to Clemson."

"And you'll go back to Florida this fall to be with her again?"

"I don't know," Luke said. "You're acting like this is some lifelong commitment I'm making to you or her. Janice doesn't think that way, why should you? Why can't we simply enjoy the here-and-now?"

"I'm not willing to settle for that," I said.

I had left that evening and never gone back, to Luke's cabin or to his bed. I'd lived with Aunt Margaret until school began.

As I watched the canoe disappear around the bend in the

river, I wondered if a day would soon come when Carolyn learned a similar lesson in honesty from Luke.

BECAUSE IT WAS STILL EARLY IN THE RAFTING SEASON, THE first cluster of Tamassee River Tour rafts did not appear till past noon. All four were filled with teenage boys, probably a church youth group. Earl Wilkinson sat in the rear of the lead raft.

"Maggie May, good to see you back home," Earl shouted, then turned his attention back to the river as he plunged over Wolf Creek Falls. I wondered if Earl told his clients what they'd be passing over when they entered this sluice.

In a few minutes Allen made his way to where I waited. If his conversation with Kowalsky had brought to mind his own loss, Allen's face did not show it. He looked impassive but focused.

"Get your camera out," he said, in a no-nonsense tone. "You're about to get a chance at a really good photograph."

I took the Nikon from its case as Herb Kowalsky stepped through shallows and onto the slab of stone his daughter lay beneath. He stared into the water—alone now, no rescue workers or environmentalists or gawkers.

In photography there is no such thing as memory. The image is either caught on film or it doesn't exist. I raised the Nikon to my right eye so I might bring this instant in Herb Kowalsky's life into being. At that moment the part of me that aimed the lens cared nothing about Herb Kowalsky or his daughter or the river or federal law. I clicked the shutter again and again until my film ran out, then jammed in another roll. It's only about light and angle and texture, I told myself. Whatever these photos do for me or anyone else is not a motive. I'm just an observer, showing what's already there.

Gnats circled Kowalsky's head and I saw him blink his right eye several times in quick succession. He raised his index finger to brush one of the insects from his eye, and I took a last photograph.

CHAPTER 5

"Did you tell Miller he'd be talking not only to a journalist of the first rank but a newly certified expert on western Carolina barbecue?" Allen asked, as we drove back up the logging road. "That was part of your job, to convince him I'm an all-around great guy so he'll feel privileged to be in my presence."

"It's too late for that," I said, doing my best to match Allen's playful tone. "Luke's read *Death and Life in Rwanda*. He says you're a sentimentalist."

We came to the end of the road. No vehicles were coming in either direction but Allen kept his foot on the brake. He glanced in the rearview mirror, as if Luke had uttered the words from the backseat.

"What did he mean by that crack?" Allen asked.

Never underestimate the egos of journalists, I reminded myself. Especially Pulitzer finalists.

I repeated what Luke had said about the wider lens that took in the past and the probable future of the massacred.

Allen shook his head slightly as I spoke. His lips clamped shut and held.

"It's nothing to get huffy about," I said. "Luke believes most people are sentimentalists."

"I'm not being huffy. It just pisses me off when people who never witnessed that kind of suffering try to shrug it off with some utilitarian strategy learned in philosophy class."

"But he has seen it," I said. "He was in the Peace Corps for eighteen months."

"But not in Africa," Allen said.

"Yes, Biafra to be exact. Or at least what used to be called Biafra. He was there during the worst of the famines."

"It was a different situation," Allen said brusquely.

Allen lifted his foot from the brake, and I half expected him to floor the accelerator and leave a plume of dust rising where he swerved off the dirt and onto the blacktop. Instead, he pulled out slowly, keeping silent as we headed back to the motel.

So the loss you've suffered hasn't purified you into some kind of cross-bearing martyr after all, I thought. *You can·be just as petty and jealous and vain as the rest of us.*

And what I felt was relief, because since my Internet foray I'd had trouble seeing myself making any kind of real connection with Allen. I'd formed a picture of a man who had suffered on a level I couldn't claim for myself in my most self-pitying moments. Yet he hadn't seemed to let it embitter him. From what I knew he hadn't turned to alcohol or drugs.

If anything, he'd appeared a candidate for sainthood. But now I saw he was still human. Human enough that I, made neither noble nor forgiving by my own past, could believe we might not be so unalike after all.

I saw Luke's truck parked in front of Mama Tilson's.

"Luke's waiting," I said. Allen flicked on the right blinker, turned into the motel parking lot, and eased close to his room door.

"I guess we'd better get on over there then," Allen said.

"I think it's best if you two had some one-on-one time," I said. "Besides, I need to check in. I'll be over a little later."

"You're not staying with your father?"

"No. One night is enough."

Allen took the keys from the ignition.

"Can you leave those with me?" I asked. "My stuff is in the trunk."

Allen handed me the keys but didn't get out. He attempted a smile.

"Sorry to get huffy, but Miller hit a nerve."

"You're not the first. If pissing people off were an Olympic sport, Luke would be a Gold Medalist."

"But what he said, especially since he's been there—it's not as easy to dismiss as I wish it were." He put his hand on the car door but then paused. "I just don't want to believe the world's that bleak."

I wanted as badly as I'd wanted anything in a long time to wrap my hand around Allen's upper arm and lean my head against his shoulder. Maybe I would have if he'd stayed a few moments longer, but he opened the door.

"See you in a little while," he said.

BEFORE I LEFT MY MOTEL ROOM I PUT ON BLUSH AND LIPSTICK, something I hadn't done often in the last year. I sprayed some perfume on my wrists and rubbed it on my neck. I looked in the mirror a last time and walked on over to Mama Tilson's.

Allen and Luke sat in the back booth. Mama Tilson had taken their plates away and refilled the tea glasses. The tape recorder lay on the table between them.

"Just in time for the supporting-materials portion of my presentation," Luke said.

I sat beside Allen and ordered while Luke removed papers and photos from a manila envelope, slid a stapled set of pages across the table.

"Wild and Scenic River regulations," Luke said. "I've underlined the relevant parts."

Luke handed Allen an eight-by-eleven black-and-white.

"In case Maggie didn't do her job. They widened the trail so reporters and the search-and-rescue squad had easier access. Clear violation of federal law."

Luke handed a final piece of paper across the table.

"That's the silt level in Licklog Creek since Bryan built his development. That stream had reproducing brook trout in it three years ago. Now you'd be lucky to find a knottyhead."

"So why didn't you report him?" Allen asked.

Luke looked at me and shook his head. Despite our conversation on the river, despite what had happened eight summers ago, Luke still believed I was on his side. I wondered if that showed faith in me or faith in himself.

"We did, both Forest Watch and the Sierra Club, and Bryan got fined a thousand dollars. It's cheaper for Bryan to pay the fine than put up the barriers to keep silt from washing into the stream. He's a businessman. It's all bottom line for him."

"Some people would say you're making him into nothing more than a caricature," Allen said. "Some people would say you and your cause lose credibility when you make things that black and white."

But that's also what appeals to people, I almost blurted out, that at least there is one thing in their lives that is black and white, all complexity drained away.

"Some people would say that, wouldn't they," Luke said, locking his eyes on Allen's. "I've read enough enviro books and seen enough lame movies to know developers are always the stock villains come to take Grandma's farm or build a housing project over a nuclear waste dump. The beauty of Bryan is he's the word made flesh. Your worst fears about developers are not just confirmed but transcended. Sometimes I can't believe him myself. He's so *pure*, the same way a shark or a cockroach is pure because it no longer needs to evolve— it's achieved perfection."

Luke paused as Momma Tilson set my food and tea on the table.

"At first I thought Bryan couldn't be that bad either," he continued. "When I traced the silt in Licklog to the development, I went to his office. I was on my best behavior. No name-calling. I didn't threaten anything. All I did was suggest he put up barriers between his construction area and the stream. When I'd finished talking the bastard opened his billfold and took out three hundred-dollar bills. That was his solution."

"Bryan says he brings jobs to this area," Allen said.

"A few short-term construction hires, though the companies he uses are from Columbia and bring most of their own people. There's some minimum-wage work as security guards and groundskeepers. Sometimes his clients need someone to mop floors or unclog a toilet. All in all, Bryan's offering great career opportunities for the folks of Oconee County."

The front door opened and Randy and Ronny came in with their wives, Jill and Nadine. The children were with them, running ahead of their parents to claim certain seats. Jill and Nadine wore slacks and blouses, but the twins were dressed in overalls and brogans. They had probably left the river and gone straight to their orchards. The two families filled the table at the room's center.

Unlike Billy, the twins had never left the county, not even for school. Nor had Jill and Nadine. The life they always imagined for themselves was marriage right after high school. They had aged quicker than I had and not just from bearing and raising children. Long hours spent helping their husbands in the orchards had lined and weathered their faces. Jill and Nadine looked tired, but they also looked happy as they got the kids seated and settled.

Don't sentimentalize their lives, I told myself. Don't believe this little Norman Rockwell portrait is necessarily anything more than a brief respite. Still, I could not help thinking how, if things had turned out differently, Ben and I might have brought our own families here on Friday nights.

Luke leaned back and raised his arms, letting them spread across the back of the booth, as if to see Allen from a wider angle.

"This is not about that girl's body being in the river."

"Then what is it about?" Allen asked.

"It's about whether federal law can be circumnavigated. Once a precedent is set, there'll be other exceptions. Bryan understands that. Why else would he be helping Kowalsky and Brennon?"

"You don't think publicity about the Tamassee being this dangerous worries him?"

"Total bullshit. Most of Bryan's clientele have their hands full getting in and out of their bathtubs. They're not getting into that river under the best of conditions."

Luke paused.

"If anybody has to worry about clientele it's Earl Wilkinson. His customers want the illusion of danger, not the real thing. They read about a place on the river so bad it'll not only kill you but won't give your body up, they'll choose to get their weekend thrills risking mall traffic instead."

Luke checked his watch.

"I've got to go in a minute. Someone from the Sierra Club's supposed to call me at eight."

He turned and leaned slightly in my direction, shutting Allen out of his line of vision. His tone was almost conspiratorial.

"I'm tempted to tell them to stay out of this."

"Why is that?" Allen asked. He wasn't going to allow himself to be left out of the conversation. "I'd think you'd want all the help you can get."

Luke glanced at Allen, the irritation clear in his eyes, his voice.

"Too many tenured college professors, too many old hippies working for Microsoft. They assuage their consciences for selling out by joining Sierra Club or Amnesty International. They've become a new-millennium version of the Optimists Club."

I laid down my fork. "That's not fair," I said. "You'd never have gotten the Wild and Scenic status without their help. You didn't have a problem calling on them then to help you. And they did help you, not just with donations but a lot of time spent making phone calls and writing letters."

"But this is different," Luke said. "They'll have to take a stand where not everyone is going to pat them on the head and say how beneficent and conscientious they are. It will take guts to say what they know is right."

"And what is that?" Allen asked.

"That the girl's body is the Tamassee's now, that the moment she stepped in the shallows she accepted the river on its own terms. That's what wilderness is—nature on its terms, not ours, and there's no middle ground. It either is or it isn't. Look at the Smokies. They've got restaurants and hotels and first-aid stations and gift shops in there. You'd think it was the North Carolina branch of Disney World. If that park was set up the way it should be, there wouldn't be a single road.

You'd walk in. There wouldn't be a McDonald's every hundred yards in case you got hungry or thirsty. And if little Johnny got lost and starved to death or was bitten by a rattlesnake, that's the price of admission."

"So why didn't you let Billy's nephew drown?"

I turned to Allen.

"Billy's nephew fell out of a canoe in Bull Sluice. There was a hydraulic. Not as bad as the one at Wolf Cliff but bad enough. It took Luke two tries."

"I didn't have to harm the river to get him out," Luke said.

"So you would have let him drown if saving him had hurt the Tamassee?"

"Yes," Luke said tersely, slipping the photos back in the envelope.

"I don't believe that," I said. "I believe you'd have gone in anyway."

"Believe what you want," Luke said, and looked at Allen. "One last thing—Maggie's cousin is right. If Brennon thinks a five-foot-high piece of polyurethane can stop the Tamassee this time of year, he has no more idea of what that river can do than Ruth Kowalsky did."

Luke eased out of the booth. He paused as he stepped past me, his right hand patting my shoulder.

"So when did you start wearing perfume and makeup, Maggie?" he said, then turned to walk out the door.

Allen clicked off the tape recorder.

"Get what you needed?" I asked.

"For sure."

"What did you talk about before I got here?"

"Mainly how hard it had been getting Wild and Scenic status for the Tamassee, not just on a state and federal level but local as well. The number of times he'd been beaten up by loggers. The number of times his home and business got shot up."

"Did Luke tell you he never reported what happened to him? Once he got beat up so bad he was in the hospital four days but wouldn't give names when Sheriff Cantrell interviewed him."

"He didn't tell me that. Was he afraid to give names?"

"No. He was proving he couldn't be intimidated. The loggers would never admit it, but they respect him for that, even if some of them hate his guts."

One of the twins' children shrieked as her drink spilled. Mama Tilson rushed over with a rag and cleaned up the mess. The child started crying and Randy lifted her into his lap, talking to her softly until she calmed down. He took a napkin and wiped the tears from her face.

"Luke really did do more than anybody else to get the river Wild and Scenic status. He wrote the majority of the letters and got the petitions signed and mailed. He got people to meetings and brought the major environmental organizations on board. The locals, not just the loggers but even folks on his side, underestimated him."

"Why?"

"Because he'd only been living here a year. Most people didn't take him seriously at first. They figured he'd get tired or scared or decide to move somewhere he could live above poverty level."

"So Luke's not a native. I thought he was."

"No, he grew up in Florida. He's been up here so long now most folks don't know or have forgotten."

I lifted the last of my apple cobbler into my mouth and set my spoon down. Randy walked over to the jukebox, his daughter held in the crook of one arm. He gave the child a quarter and let her drop it into the money slot. Dwight Yoakam's high lonesome wail soon filled the room.

"Did you talk any about Africa?" I asked.

"I brought it up, but Luke said he'd come to talk about the Tamassee."

I pushed the empty bowl to the center of the table. The walk into and out of the gorge had sharpened my appetite.

"So what else did Luke have to say?"

"A few things about you. I hadn't realized what an environmental warrior you once were."

"In all my tie-dyed glory."

"He told me your mother died during your junior year. He told me what happened to your brother."

Allen looked at Randy's daughter perched in her father's lap. She tapped a plastic straw against Randy's leg as she sang along with the jukebox. I wondered if Allen saw something that reminded him of Miranda, if not of how she had been then something of what she might have become. I recalled what my art history teacher had told our class about Rembrandt. Three of his children died before reaching adulthood, and later in life Rembrandt drew them as he imagined they would have been as adults.

"Luke asked if we were lovers," Allen said, still looking at Randy's daughter.

"Why would he think that?"

Allen looked at me now, his eyes meeting mine.

"Maybe because I was clearly interested in what he had to say about you."

Claire Pritchard-Hemphill's face surfaced in my mind. I suddenly wondered if there was something about me that reminded Allen of her. Certainly it wasn't my appearance—I was pure Appalachia via Northern Europe Celt, my features bleached out by generations of cold, sunless days, my eyes an icy shade of blue. But maybe a gesture or mannerism, maybe my voice or the shampoo I used. It was a silly notion but also a disturbing one.

"I hope that's okay," he said, "that I'm interested in you. If it's not—"

"It's okay," I interrupted. "It's more than okay."

I laid my hand on the table, close enough to Allen's that he could easily place his hand on mine. But he didn't. Give him time, I thought.

I nodded at Ronny and Randy's table. "You talked to the Moseley brothers this morning, I guess."

"A little. They didn't have a lot to say."

"That's the way they are, especially around people they don't know well."

"You grew up with them?"

"Yes. Their wives too. As a matter of fact, I've got some catching up with them I want to do. Why don't you wait for me over at the motel. Let me talk to them a little while, maybe get you a good quote, then I'll show you a few local sights, give you a chance to hear some good picking and singing. That is, if you're interested."

"Definitely," Allen said, and picked up the bill.

BONDING FIRES ORIGINATED IN THE SCOTTISH MIDLANDS. A family's hearth fire was never allowed to die down completely. Banked embers from the previous night's fire were stirred and kindled back into flames. When children left to marry and raise their own families, they took fire from their parents' hearth with them. It was both heirloom and talisman, nurtured and protected because generations recognized it for what it was—living memory. When some clans emigrated they kept the fires burning on the ships as they crossed the Atlantic. Then they hauled them up into the southern Appalachians from Charleston or down the Shenandoah from Philadelphia. There had been one bonding fire started in the 1500s that was kept alive until the 1970s. The flame was tended by an old man and extinguished only when a dam flooded the valley where he'd lived eight decades. Two hundred feet of water covered that hearth now.

The closest thing to a bonding fire in Tamassee was Saturday night at Billy's store. It was not unusual to see four generations of the same family seated in lawn chairs together, not fire but song passed from parent to child.

Lou Henson began the communal gatherings the summer I

turned fourteen. Ben hadn't wanted to go, so Aunt Margaret, who had planned to drive, offered to stay with Ben while the rest of us went. But Daddy wouldn't hear of it.

"Nobody notices those burns but you," Daddy said to Ben, and his voice was angry and frustrated, as if the scars were just something in Ben's imagination. "You'll go whether you want to or not. I'll not let you hide in the house and feel sorry for yourself. You hear?"

Daddy was shouting but Momma said nothing. It was Aunt Margaret who placed her hand firmly on Daddy's arm.

"I'll go," Ben had said softly, just as he did the other times Daddy insisted he attend a family reunion or a gospel singing or—worst of all because people didn't know him there—go down to Seneca.

When Daddy went to get his cap, Aunt Margaret leaned over me.

"Your daddy isn't mad at Ben, honey. He's mad at himself." But if that was true, I thought, why was he yelling at Ben?

My girlfriends and I were beginning to be interested in the boys in our middle-school classes. They lagged behind us physically and socially, but despite their attempts to act otherwise, we knew they were interested in us as well. We would drag them out in front of the pumps to dance. They'd be awkward as newborn colts and all blushing but you could tell they enjoyed our attention. Sometimes the bolder boys would venture a kiss or slip their hands under shirts or blouses to caress the small of our backs, and we realized they were catching up to us perhaps faster than we were quite ready for.

I'd be out there enjoying myself and then I'd turn and see

Ben in the shadows, not staying in one place but always keeping within the perimeter of the lit-up storefront, like a hungry stray dog circling a hunter's campfire. And I'd think, What right do I have to enjoy myself when he can't? Sometimes I'd go join him, and we'd wait together until Momma and Daddy were ready to go. Other times I wouldn't. Every now and then Momma would coax Ben out with soft drinks and food, but he quickly returned to the shadows.

BY THE TIME ALLEN AND I GOT TO THE STORE A FEW DOZEN people had gathered, and I knew a name to match every face. Billy was on the porch with his sons, setting up a makeshift stage for Randall and Jeff Alexander. Billy's wife Wanda worked the cash register inside. Most people had brought lawn chairs, though a few sat on the gas islands.

"You want a beer?" Allen asked.

"Yes. Something in a bottle."

I reached into my jeans for some money.

"I got it," Allen said.

I looked around at the familiar faces, familiar but older. Several people waved or nodded. Randall and Jeff arrived, instrument cases in their right hands, Randall's left hand on his son's elbow. They stepped slowly up the steps, Jeff holding on to the banister. Jeff led his father to a stool and then uncased the instruments. He handed his father the guitar.

Joel's pickup pulled off onto the shoulder of the road. He lifted two lawn chairs from the truck bed and helped Aunt Margaret out of the passenger side.

"Oh, girl, it's so good to see you," Aunt Margaret said, pulling me to her. She was Daddy's older sister but had always looked and seemed younger, even more so since Daddy had been sick. "It seems like it's been more than forever."

I knew without looking that Aunt Margaret's eyes had brightened with tears as she hugged me tighter. In a few moments she loosened her arms and stepped back to look at me.

"You're pretty as ever, Maggie," she said, clasping her hand around mine. "Come here." We stepped farther away from the stage where she could speak more softly. "I don't know what your daddy's telling you, but he's in a bad way now. That cancer's eating away at him."

Aunt Margaret gave my hand a final squeeze. I felt the strength in that hand.

"The time's come to let bygones be bygones, Maggie," she said. "You wait too long, and you'll not have a chance to set things right."

"Yes ma'am," I said, because it was the easy response. But I also knew if Aunt Margaret were in my place she would do exactly what she was telling me to do. Ben had inherited that forgiving nature. I had not.

Randall and Jeff started into "Mary of the Wild Moor," so we turned to face the porch as Jeff began to sing.

It was on one cold winter's night
The winds blew across the wild moor,
Mary came wandering home with her babe
Till she came to her father's door.

After the second verse Randall took a solo. I watched the blur of his fingers as they plucked and bent the strings. I tried to imagine what it would be like to know something as well as Randall Alexander knew that guitar without being able to see it, to know it only by feel. As I watched the old man lean his head toward the strings as if in some private conversation, I wondered if sight would be just another distraction, a barrier to that place inside the music where nothing and no one could break through.

Allen joined us, two long-necked Budweisers in one hand and a bag of boiled peanuts in the other. I introduced him to Aunt Margaret and Joel, but it was hard to talk over the music, so we soon turned back to watch Randall and Jeff. Aunt Margaret and Joel sat down in their chairs. Allen and I moved closer to the porch to sit on the gas island.

"I've heard some of these ballads date back to Elizabethan times," Allen said, when the song ended. "Some of the language up here as well."

"That gets exaggerated a good bit. People come up here expecting to wander into a Shakespeare play. But there's some truth to it. Some of the old words and ways have held on."

Randall and Jeff began playing again, a faster song. More people had arrived, their vehicles parked up and down the road. Billy never advertised these gatherings. There was no need.

"They're good," Allen said, when Randall and Jeff took a break. "Especially the father."

"He used to do some session work in Nashville. But he's about given that up now."

I set my empty bottle beside Allen's.

"You want another?" he asked.

"Sure, if you're having one."

Allen looked at the mound of peanut shells at my feet and smiled.

"I'll get some more peanuts too. But I'm holding the bag this time. That way I might get to eat a few."

Allen went into the store as Billy stepped off the porch to talk to Aunt Margaret. It took a couple of minutes, but he finally got her up to join Randall and Jeff, who were back on the stools tuning their instruments.

Allen handed me my beer and sat down, closer, his leg touching mine as Randall and Jeff played the intro to "Omie Wise."

Not for the first time, it occurred to me that sorrow could be purified into song the same way a piece of coal is purified into a diamond.

> *Come listen to my story*
> *About Omie Wise*
> *And how she was deluded*
> *By John Lewis's lies.*

And as I heard Aunt Margaret's voice again I remembered the Sunday mornings in church, Preacher Tilson, red-faced from shouting and pacing back and forth, the Bible raised above his head. I remembered the shouts and tears, the speaking in tongues, and how frightening it all was. Until Aunt Margaret stood beside the rickety piano and sang.

I was no longer afraid then. Her voice settled over me like a warm balm. Sometimes as she sang I'd look out the open window and see the gravestones and wonder if even the dead listened.

Randall and Jeff broke into brief instrumental solos midsong, then let the sounds of the guitar and banjo flow back together smoothly as two streams merging while Aunt Margaret reached the song's most chilling verses.

Oh pity your poor infant
And spare me my life.
Let me go rejected
And not be your wife.
No pity, no pity,
John Lewis did cry.
On deep river's bottom
Your body will lie.

I thought of Ruth Kowalsky in the blackness of the undercut, and I thought of her parents in their motel room in Seneca. Did they talk of their loss or turn on the TV or merely wait in silence? I wondered what Allen had done those first days after he'd lost his family. Had he sought solitude or friends or work? Had he gone into a bar or a church? Had he been able to stay in a house as much his wife and daughter's as it was his?

And I thought of my own family those first weeks after Ben came home from the hospital, how, when we ate our meals, hardly anyone talked or raised their eyes from the plates, making it worse for Ben, who was already getting taunted at school. What must he have thought when it seemed his own family could not bear to look at him? It was like we were all ashamed for our parts in what had happened. Momma would try to say something, maybe ask what Ben and I learned in our classes, but every question and answer was in syllables, not sentences. Those first weeks Daddy ate quickly and left for Henson's Store as soon as he could. When he came back, there was always beer on his breath.

One of those nights Daddy came back and went directly into Ben's bedroom. Unlike me, Ben was already asleep. Daddy didn't turn on the light. He woke Ben up with his voice, talking so loud I could hear him as well.

"Soon as you get that next skin graft you'll be as handsome a fellow as Rock Hudson," Daddy said.

Then he'd stumbled on down the hall. I lay in bed and vowed again what I'd been vowing since the accident—that I'd study hard and get a college scholarship so I could make a life far beyond Tamassee.

"Do you have any of her singing ability?" Allen asked, when Aunt Margaret finished.

"No. She's the only one in our family with that kind of gift."

Randall and Jeff started a slow song and several couples got up to dance. I stood and reached for Allen's hand.

"Come on."

Allen stood up reluctantly. "I grew up Southern Baptist. We have an eleventh commandment: Thou shalt not dance."

I took his hand. "No excuses," I said.

I led Allen to the open area that served as a dance floor. I placed his arms around me and pulled him closer, my head against his chest. I felt him tense as my right hand pressed the small of his back. I closed my eyes and breathed in the smell of soap and lime aftershave.

We didn't move much, just swayed in each other's arms. Allen's right hand did not urge me closer. He still wanted some distance between us.

We danced one more time, then got in the car and headed toward the motel, but Allen did not turn in. He drove on toward the river, pulling off at the parking lot on the South Carolina side. We walked out to the middle of the bridge and leaned against the concrete railing.

After a couple of minutes he spoke. "Did the Moseleys say anything about the recovery?"

"We talked mainly about who's gotten married, who's divorced, that kind of thing. We didn't talk about the other until we were in the parking lot and the kids out of hearing range."

A pickup with Georgia plates drove slowly across the bridge, its truck bed filled with fertilizer bags. The bridge trembled from its weight.

"They didn't have a lot to say, just that Kowalsky didn't understand they were doing everything possible. The twins take a lot of pride in being professionals. It bothers them that Kowalsky thinks they're incompetent."

"Phillips probably feels the same way," Allen said. "I couldn't get him to say much, especially with Brennon and Kowalsky nearby, but you can tell the poor guy would love to wake up and realize this is all a bad dream. He's getting pressure from all sides."

A fisherman's lantern flickered downstream near the bend of the river.

"Are we still planning to leave in the morning, or do you need to talk to some more people?"

"No, I've got enough," Allen said. "Now it's just a matter of writing the thing."

"So what time do you want to leave?"

"The sooner the better. Lee wants a thousand to fifteen hundred words. If you don't mind, I may let you drive so I can work on it going back."

"Sure."

"You want to aim for nine?"

"That sounds good," I said.

A breeze rose up off the river. Only the sun's rim showed above Whiteside Mountain. The temperature would fall quickly now. No matter how warm the day had been, it would be blanket weather tonight. For a few minutes the only sound was the river rubbing against rocks. Then from the deep woods near Chestnut Ridge came something else, a sound like a crying child.

"What's that?" Allen asked.

"A bobcat would be my guess, though Billy might argue it's his cougar."

"You want me to go get my tape recorder?" Allen asked.

"If it comes closer. Right now it's too far away to pick up."

"When were cougars last here—I mean, verified?"

"One was killed with its two kittens in 1908."

"Do you think Billy really saw one?"

"I don't know. When you're a kid you can see most any-thing, I suppose. Billy believes he saw it, I don't doubt that."

The day's last light momentarily settled on Sassafras Moun-tain before its slide down the mountain's west slope. We lis-tened until that light was extinguished, but what had cried out in the deep woods stayed silent.

This is as good a time as you may get, I told myself, then spoke. "I did an Internet search on you this morning. I hadn't known what had happened."

I couldn't see Allen's reaction, but he paused a few seconds before speaking. "Nobody at the paper knew except Hudson. I wanted it that way."

"Why?"

"Because other people don't know how to deal with it. They'll be talking about children or spouses and suddenly switch the subject as soon as you show up. Everybody in the office sees family pictures but you. If that's not happening it's the opposite, which is worse. They believe you need to spill your guts to somebody, usually themselves, but if not them some psychiatrist or therapy group they know of. Either way, it just makes things worse."

"I won't do that to you," I said.

"Good. I do want us to be open about it. I almost said something at supper."

"Why didn't you?"

"I'm still not sure what I feel—what I should feel—about Claire. That and I wasn't sure how you would react."

"How so?"

"It might make you leery of me."

"I don't scare easy," I said, trying to sound surer than I perhaps was.

"Good."

Below, a trout snatched something off the surface. Another splash came from farther downstream, a sure sign mayflies or caddis flies were hatching.

"And what about you?" Allen asked. "Have you been married?"

"No."

"Come close?"

"Not really," I said. "I was semi-serious about a guy in Laurens, but he decided I had major character defects."

"What defects?"

"Self-righteousness. Shutting myself off from others. *Emotional frigidity*, to use his term. When I'd told him my past had a lot to do with that, he argued I'd have been the same if Ben and I hadn't been burned, if Momma hadn't died. He said I liked the way I was. Having someone or something else to blame just made it easier for me not to change."

"Do you think he was right?"

"I didn't at the time."

"That's a pretty open-ended answer."

"Let's leave it open-ended. That way you can decide on your own."

"What about your relationship with Luke?"

"Luke's not the marrying kind."

"But you loved him?"

"Yes. But it was a naïve kind of love. I didn't realize some-one could take your love but not necessarily love you back."

"I see," Allen said, and I felt his hand settle on the small of my back. He brought me close and we kissed. We stayed on the bridge a while longer, then drove back to the motel. I went to my room and changed into my pajamas. I got com-fortable in the bed, Kephart's *Our Southern Highlanders* in my hands, but instead of reading I thought about earlier that eve-ning when dark blurred the river with the bank and trees. I remembered how the river was only a sound whispering below us as Allen and I stood on a bridge connecting two states, and how, at least for a while, I did not think of Ruth Kowalsky's body a mile downstream waiting to be raised, or think of my father dying a little more as he sat in his house alone.

I wondered if I might hear a light knock on my motel room's door, and if that knock came what I would say, what I would do. But Allen Hemphill did not knock on my door, so I lay the book on the night table and cut off the lamp.

Part Two

"I'm going up to Lou's a minute to get some cigarettes," Daddy had said. "You look after your brother till I get back." Mama had gone with Aunt Margaret to buy canning jars in Seneca, leaving Ben and me with Daddy, telling him to watch us and the pot of beans she'd left simmering on the stove. But Daddy needed his cigarettes, so he left us there in the front room, Ben on the floor playing with a toy train and me in a chair doing math homework. After a few minutes Ben said, "I'm hungry," and got up while I added a last column of figures and wrote down the answer. Only a few seconds passed before I followed him into the kitchen, but Ben's hand was already on the handle, his arm trembling as he pulled the two-gallon pot of beans off the eye, my arm reaching out for the handle but too late as scalding water and beans poured

onto Ben's face and my left arm and leg. For a few moments I didn't know the water had scalded me as well, because it was like I'd cast every sense and emotion out of myself and across the two-foot space between Ben and me, done this because sight alone wasn't enough to comprehend what had happened to my brother. How could it be otherwise when only the eyes Ben had closed at the last instant were saved.

Neither of us screamed. Ben just whimpered and then not even that while I didn't make a sound because it was like watching a movie, no more real than that because Ben's ruined face couldn't be real. The room tilted and a wave of blackness rushed in. When the floor leveled again and the room lightened, Ben and I were holding on to each other in the kitchen corner, as if the beans spilled on the floor could still hurt us. Ben's pain was dimmed by shock, but my arm and leg now burned as though I was on fire, a fire that spread to cover my whole body, invisible flames that never quit burning. "The wicked are their own wick" was how Reverend Tilson described hell the morning he lit a candle in church and had us pass it around as he preached. That was exactly what I felt, what I saw when I closed my eyes—a candlewick inside an unquenchable flame. If older or in less pain I might have been able to clear my head enough to telephone Uncle Mark or Billy's parents. But that was beyond me. All I could do was watch the clock on the stove, because the red second hand proved that time still moved and that meant Daddy had to come back and Ben and I wouldn't be huddled in that corner forever. But it was forever. Daddy had been talking with Lou Henson and forgotten about us being alone. I counted out loud each time the second hand passed the twelve, telling myself that before the hand reached that twelve again Daddy would be back. I had reached twenty-seven before I heard Daddy's truck.

"What kind of mess have you made, girl?" Daddy said, when he saw the spilled beans and Ben and me huddled in the corner. Saying those words to me as he stared at the beans and the pot, not really seeing us until Ben heard Daddy's voice and turned his face and Daddy saw. Then a few more moments or minutes lost because we were no longer in the house but in the truck and Ben not making a sound, so quiet I believed he was dying. Each time the road curved we slid back and forth across the front seat and the pain leaped up and covered my arm and leg whenever I bumped against Ben or the door. All the while thinking, My brother is dying, and finally saying it out loud, and Daddy saying, "You shush now," and not saying anything else as he jerked the steering wheel with one hand and shifted gears with the other. As we swung through those curves the dropoffs fell away below us for what seemed miles, and I thought between surges of pain that we were going to fall into the sky and never stop falling.

The road finally straightened when we came off the mountain. I looked at Ben and his eyes were barely open, his lashes flickering, and I suddenly knew certain as anything in my life that if he did close his eyes he'd never open them again. "Don't close your eyes, Ben," I said, and his eyes looked back at me but unfocused, like I'd just woken him up. I kept telling him to keep his eyes open even as the hospital orderlies lifted him and me out of the cab and they took him toward one room and me to another, Daddy going with Ben and leaving me alone until Momma got there. *The doctor had my arm and leg bandaged by then and Momma thanked him and took me not home but to the waiting room. "I've got to see how Ben is doing," she told me.*

"I want to go too," I said, but Momma just shook her head. Grown-ups I did not know sat in the chairs that lined the walls, dressed as though in a church, and as quiet. Not one of them looked like they wanted to be there. The woman across from me stared at the bandages on my arm. She whispered something to the man next to her and he stared at the bandages as well. They did not smile at me or look sad or sympathetic. They just stared. To be left in this room is part of your punishment, I said to myself.

I rode back with Daddy because Momma was staying with Ben. Once home I walked alone out to the far pasture, my arm gauzed, no blazing pain now, just a low simmer. I looked at the mountains and felt at ten what I would find a word for only years later—claustrophobic. Because it felt as though the mountains had moved closer together since we'd been at the hospital, and would keep on moving closer until they finally suffocated me.

CHAPTER 6

Under a darkroom safelight everything is gray. Your hands are drained of life. Stop bath settles in your nostrils and stomach like formaldehyde. Maybe that's the way it should be, because what a photograph does is embalm something or someone into a boxed and stilled forever.

A darkroom is a place where your failures come to light: a wrong combination of f-stop and shutter speed, a misjudgment of depth of field or right exposure. Or you make new errors. You don't check the temperature of the chemicals; something spills; you turn the white light on too soon.

But sometimes, everything happens just as it should. You rinse the print in the darkroom's gray light, and there in your hands is the photograph you hoped for.

And that is what happened on Monday afternoon when I lifted the five-by-seven from the print dryer and stepped out of the darkroom with the other pictures worth showing to Lee. I sat down at my desk to study the photograph more closely. Everything was right—light, shutter speed, symmetry.

Wolf Cliff Falls dominated the frame, the backdrop all water and rock. Herb Kowalsky stood slightly to the right. No one else was in the photo. My shot angled upward out of the pool, ending not far above Kowalsky's head. Such a perspective usually makes a person seem larger than life, able to dominate a scene. But in this photograph the angle only emphasized Kowlasky's powerlessness, juxtaposed as he was next to the falls that held his daughter.

Nevertheless, you could make out that Kowalsky was staring into the water, and you could see the index finger raised to brush away a tear that had not existed until this moment.

"Sweet Jesus," Lee said, when I showed him the photograph. "That's the father?"

"Yes."

"Oh, man, this is good, Maggie. This is real good."

Lee went to his door and shouted for Phil.

"Check this out," Lee said, handing the photograph to Phil. "Maggie's kicking your ass."

Phil laid the picture on Lee's desk as though reading an article.

"Hell of a photo," he said. "This is one to nominate for awards, Lee."

"Damn straight," Lee said, nodding his head for emphasis.

"You're telling me nothing I don't know. You'd have to be blind not to see this is a great photo."

He turned to me.

"You shown it to Hemphill yet?"

"No."

"Well, why don't you? Maybe it will inspire him to get his article done. He's got less than a day and I haven't seen word one."

"Okay," I said.

I left Lee and Phil and took the elevator to the second floor.

"Lee thought you might want to see this," I said, handing Allen the photograph.

He stared at it with the same intensity Phil had.

"That's a hell of a picture," he finally said.

"Of course it's just a photograph," I said teasingly. "As someone I know once said, 'There is always something more that lies outside the camera's framed, mechanical truth.'"

Allen grimaced. "Where did you come across that youthful indiscretion?"

"Part of my background check."

"I got a lot of well-deserved grief about that comment," Allen said, looking embarrassed. "A photographer friend e-mailed me a bunch of Susan Sontag quotes. Another guy sent me a book of photos taken by Henri Cartier-Bresson."

"So have we won you over?"

"I don't know. I'm a lot less sure about most things than I once was." He handed the photograph back to me. "But I do know this is a damn good photo."

"It's yours as much as mine. You set it up."

"What I did was like giving a writer a possible topic. What the person does with the material makes it good or not."

I looked around Allen's office. Sparse. The walls bare. A few books on the shelves, mainly style manuals and dictionaries. On his desk the computer, beside it pens and pencils sprouting from a coffee cup. A legal pad and his tape recorder. No photographs.

"It must be nice having this kind of space," I said. "Sometimes my cubicle feels like I'm inside some kid's ant farm."

Allen pointed at the print in my hand. "A few more photographs like that one and Hudson will probably give you *his* office."

"As they say in Oconee County, that's about as likely as a toad growing wings." I glanced at the legal pad. "So how's your article coming?"

"I'm still typing."

"If you don't have time for supper tonight, I understand."

"No," Allen said. "I'm close enough, just two more paragraphs. As a matter of fact, I was going to take a coffee break before I finished up. Why don't you take it with me?"

We rode the elevator to the main lobby and were almost to the door when someone called Allen's name. Thomas Hudson stood at the doorway of his office. He waved Allen over.

"I'll be back in a minute," Allen said.

I walked out into a day that was a sure precursor of what the next four months would be. Unlike in the mountains, Columbia's air already had a weight to it, a weight made up of equal parts heat and humidity. The first time I'd gone running after moving downstate I was sweat-soaked and gasping after a half mile. It had felt like I was exercising in a sauna. Ninety-one degrees, the Bank of America sign declared.

I glanced through the glass doors and saw Allen still with Hudson. I crossed Main Street. I didn't go into Starbucks but walked three doors down to the Capital Newsstand. I wanted to see if the latest *LensWork* or *Black and White* was in.

When I came back out, Allen was waiting across the street. I waved to get his attention but he didn't see me. He turned to go back inside. I yelled his name and stepped off the curb. A horn blared as a flatbed truck passed close enough that I had to jump back and grab a parking meter so as not to fall. Close. But not so close as to warrant Allen's expression. As I regained my balance, my eyes still on his face, I wondered if Herb Kowalsky had looked much the same as he watched his daughter sweep down the river.

"I'm okay," I said, but as we sat down with our coffee a few minutes later it was clear Allen wasn't. "Lee would say I wasn't aware traffic could pass in two different directions at once."

Allen did not smile. I put my hand over his.

"Hey, it wasn't as close as it looked."

"It was close enough," Allen said. He shut his eyes for a few moments. When he opened them they looked sad, resigned.

I lifted my coffee cup and drank. Allen's cup remained untouched.

"Hey," I said, smiling but also a little exasperated. "That's all there is to it. I promise I have no Sexton or Plath volumes on my bedside table. I don't listen to Joni Mitchell CDs with my hands full of sleeping pills. I was just coming to get you and was careless."

Allen stared at the table. His free hand lifted the coffee cup from the table as though checking its weight, then placed the cup back without raising it to his lips. He cleared his throat.

"Claire was coming to get me at Dulles when she and Miranda died. The flight had been eighteen hours, and I was tired and irritable. I waited thirty minutes and then called the house, figuring she'd forgotten. The answering machine picked up. I called again fifteen minutes later and left a message this time. I told Claire I was getting a cab. I also told her that if she weren't so damn self-involved she might remember when her husband who'd been gone five weeks was coming home."

I held my hand open between us as if to deflect his words.

"You don't have to tell me this," I said.

"I know," Allen said, "but I think it's better if I do."

"Okay," I said.

"I got my taxi and we headed toward Georgetown. It was raining hard so the ride took longer than usual. On the other side of the parkway it was worse. There'd been·a wreck, and traffic was backed up a mile. I remember thinking how glad I was that the wreck was in the southbound lanes. When I got to the apartment, two messages were blinking on the answering machine. The first was mine. The second was the hospital, telling me to call immediately."

"You can't feel bad about things you didn't know," I said. My words sounded so facile I didn't say anything else. For a few moments neither of us spoke.

"Well," Allen finally said. "We better get back to work."

"I'm glad you told me," I said. "I want to know these things."

Allen lifted the coffee to his mouth. It had sat long enough that he could drink deeply. He did not put the cup down until it was empty.

"Let's go," he said.

As we stepped off the curb I held on to his arm.

"What did Hudson want?" I asked.

"Nothing much, really. He just told me he was looking forward to the article about Ruth Kowalsky."

"Must be nice," I said. "Hudson's never acknowledged anything I've ever finished, much less something I'm still working on."

"This is an exception for me as well," Allen said. "He must think this story is going to sell a lot of papers. Hudson's always struck me as a bottom-line kind of guy."

We got in the elevator and Allen pushed floors two and three.

"I look forward to dinner tonight," he said as the doors closed.

"Like I said yesterday, don't expect too much. For me cooking is more about survival than artistry."

Allen smiled. "Don't worry. Whatever you cook and however you cook it, I promise you I've eaten worse. That's one of the realities of spending time in the third world."

"I suppose my culinary skills can rise to at least those expectations."

The elevator shuddered to a stop and I stepped out. As the metal doors shut, I wished the most useless thing in the world—that I'd met Allen Hemphill before Claire Pritchard had.

"I WASN'T SURE WHICH ONE," ALLEN SAID WHEN HE ARRIVED, offering me the bottles of red and white wine he gripped in his right hand. He set a loaf of bread on the counter.

He had shaved and, like me, changed out of his work clothes. He wore brown chinos and a blue flannel shirt that matched his eyes. I suspected he too had spent more time looking in the mirror attentively than he had in a while.

"Red," I said, taking the bottles from his hand.

"Can I help do anything?"

"No, it's all taken care of, such as it is."

"How about a glass of wine?"

"Sure," I said, and lifted two glasses from the cupboard.

We went into the living room and talked about work while Emmylou Harris sang of love lost and love found. When we finished our wine Allen came to the kitchen as I cooked the pasta, but our conversation was stilted, like two people dancing but unsure of the other's next step.

As we sat down for dinner I was glad I'd loaded the CD player with five disks. At least the music filled the gaps in the conversation.

"It's not that bad, is it?" I asked, as Allen set down his fork after a few bites. I wasn't sure if I was referring to the whole evening or the food.

"No, it's very good." Allen smiled weakly. "I'm nervous, so nervous I can't eat. It's like I'm back in junior high on my first date. I couldn't eat then either." He paused. "That's what this is, isn't it, a date?"

"C'mon." I stood up and held out my hand, then led him to the couch in the living room.

Unlike our kiss on the bridge, this one lasted a good long time. I lifted my hand to his face and felt hair thicker and wavier than mine. How far do I want this to go, at least for tonight? I wondered. How far does he? Not too far, Allen's hands and lips soon made clear. Tonight at least.

After a few minutes I kicked off my shoes. I leaned my head against Allen's chest, my knees pressing the side of his leg.

"I've been wanting to ask you a question," I said, "but I'm not sure it's something you'll want to answer."

"Go ahead," Allen said. "I've spent most of my life asking people those kinds of questions, so turnabout is fair play."

"Has writing about Ruth Kowalsky been hard for you?"

Allen didn't say anything for a few moments.

"In some ways," he finally said. "It intensifies certain regrets."

"What regrets?" I asked, nuzzling closer, feeling the softness of the flannel on my cheek, the beat of his heart beneath it.

"That for a good portion of my daughter's life I wasn't even on the same continent. That she lived only nine years, and during that time she had a father who put her second to his career."

"You couldn't have known her life would be so short."

"And I'll never know if I really would have made Kosovo my last overseas assignment. That's what I told both her and her mother. I want to believe that's what I'd have done. But even if I had, that wouldn't have changed nine years of only seeing her a week out of each month, less than that for the six months I was in Rwanda."

Allen shifted so he could look at me.

"You know what she told me when she was five?"

"What?"

"That her friends had fathers they saw every day."

"That must have hurt."

"Not enough to do anything about it."

I settled back into Allen's chest.

"What about your wife. Regrets?"

"Sure, but they're different. Claire didn't need me the way Miranda did. Claire was independent. She'd made a life for herself when I wasn't around. She had her own career and friends. She was an attractive woman. There may have been other men in her life—probably were, those last two years. But I didn't blame her for that. How could I?"

"And you? Did you have other women?"

"No, though I'm not sure Claire believed that. I put all my energy into the writing. A lot of the other journalists would go out drinking and skirt-chasing, but at night I stayed in my room and wrote."

"So you were faithful to Claire," I said. It was the first time I'd spoken her name, and it unsettled me to hear it come from my mouth, almost as if I were afraid the word might invoke her spirit to join us in the room.

"Faithful to her, or maybe just faithful to the writing."

Lucinda Williams's voice filled our silence for a few moments. She sang of car wheels on a gravel road, of things left behind but not forgotten.

"That evening after I came back from the hospital, I gathered all my notes for the Kosovo book and threw them in the fireplace. I struck a match and watched them burn. I don't know why I thought that would make any difference."

Allen paused.

"But this situation with Ruth Kowalsky, it's like I've been given another chance to be a good father by helping get another man's daughter out of that river. I didn't see that at first, when Hudson asked me to do this story, but I see it now. Does that make sense?"

"Yes," I said, but I was thinking something else, that sometimes you don't get another chance.

"I used to be arrogant enough to think I could save the world, but I know better now. The best you can do is find a single good cause, no matter how small, and put all your energy into that."

"Luke says the same thing," I said. "He says that's what the Tamassee is for him."

"Because of what he saw in Biafra?"

"Yes."

"It was hands-on for him, I guess—people literally dying in his arms."

"Yes," I said. "It was."

"It wasn't that way for me. What I witnessed wasn't something I felt in a personal way. I always seemed somehow removed from it, like there was a partition between me and the victims. I used to try to rationalize that. I'd compare myself to relief workers, or ER doctors back in the United States. Like them I couldn't get emotionally involved. If I did, the suffering would overwhelm me, and what I was doing was too important to allow that to happen. That's what I told myself."

"Maybe it would have overwhelmed you. And what you did was important. People needed to know what was happening there."

The CD ended and the room was quiet except for the ticking of the chestnut mantel clock passed down to my mother from her mother. The day after Momma's funeral I'd taken it from Daddy's room and placed it on my bureau. I hadn't asked and he'd never said a word about my taking it.

"But I was little more than a voyeur. I hadn't earned the right to be 'emotionally detached.' I always arrived after the fact, and even then I wasn't the one lifting those bodies into graves. There was a girl in Kosovo who'd been killed by a land mine. She looked Miranda's age. Same complexion, same color hair. Maybe the same color of eyes if they'd been open. She lay in a potato field. It had rained and the field had been recently harvested. They searched an hour on top of and then under the mud before they found her right foot."

I wanted to say something but Allen raised his index finger as though in admonishment.

"For a few seconds I saw that this girl could be my daughter, that this was the world I lived in. I closed my eyes right there at the field's edge, and, at least for one moment, I didn't believe I could open them again. It was too awful to look at. I understood something else at that moment as well, something I'd witnessed in Cambodia—women who'd seen so many of their family members and friends die in Pol Pot's death camps that they had willed themselves blind."

He blinked as though coming out of a dream.

"And then it was like adjusting the focus on a camera. No, I told myself, this isn't my world. This has nothing to do with my reality. At that moment the partition came back up. I could see then, see the girl's body, the search for the foot. I could see it all, and it could touch me no more than if I were watching a movie."

The mantel clock chimed ten times.

"But that changed when I was in the morgue's basement and placed my hand on Miranda's cheek."

Allen looked at me.

"Do you understand what I mean? I felt death, not just observed it."

I did understand, because I was with Momma when she died. I had been on one side of the bed and Ben on the other. The doctor had seen her that morning and told us she'd live another day or two, but by early evening her breaths short-ened to harsh gasps. Daddy called an ambulance and then called Aunt Margaret. He stayed in the room only until she arrived.

"I can't watch her die," he told her. "I just can't." He waited on the porch till it was over. But Aunt Margaret was there with us, talking to Momma in a soothing voice, her hand brushing Momma's hair. Then Momma exhaled one last time, almost like a sigh. I lifted Momma's wrist to feel her pulse, and her arm felt heavier, as though death gave a body an additional weight to carry.

The blue in Allen's eyes seemed brighter, like the blue you see when long-cured firewood burns. I knew he had never told anyone what he was telling me now.

"Yes," I said. "I understand."

"When I felt Miranda's cheek I realized the Bible is right about us being made of clay, because that was what she felt like—cool, clammy. I lifted her off the morgue table, and as I held her she felt so solid. And every dead body I'd seen in Cambodia and Rwanda and Kosovo suddenly had solidity as well. So does Ruth Kowalsky's."

I listened to time clicking like hooves on pavement. But time isn't something you can rein in. It moves on without pause, taking us with it no matter how much we wish otherwise.

Allen's attention was now on the clock as well. A wry smile flickered on his face.

"I'm so glad we could have such lighthearted fun on our first date. Maybe next time we can read aloud passages from *Blood Meridian*."

"I haven't read that one."

"Classic Cormac McCarthy. In other words, four hundred pages of unrelenting bleakness. It's like falling into a well with no bottom. You keep thinking the book can't get any darker, but it always does."

Allen checked the clock again.

"I need to go," he said.

We kissed, a final lingering kiss, and I walked him to the door.

"This is good," he said, "being with you, I mean. But a little scary, too, like what I'm feeling is happening a little too fast and part of me hasn't caught up yet."

"I know," I said, touching Allen's face with my left hand. "Wherever this is going between us, there's no rush to get there."

I closed the door and started clearing the table. Don't expect too much, I cautioned myself. But I put on another CD, and as I washed the dishes I sang along.

WHEN THE DOCTORS AT THE BURN UNIT IN COLUMBIA HAD done all they could, when all the skin grafts had been completed, it hadn't been enough. The taunts and stares and the nicknames Ben had been given by classmates, the middle school and high school ball games and dances Daddy made him attend, the nights he stayed in his room listening to songs about things he must have believed he'd never experience, all of that he had endured, never acknowledging the pain he felt to Daddy or Momma or me.

Daddy always made it worse. Before every skin graft he

would tell Ben this one was going to make all the difference. When it didn't make much of a difference at all, Daddy would insist it had, though you could see the disappointment in his eyes even as he said it. And still he couldn't keep himself from going into a rage when he'd find Ben in his room nights there was a ball game or dance. You'd think Ben wanted to stay in his room just to spite him, and all the while Momma saying nothing.

And Ben never telling Daddy to go to hell or even saying no. When I tried to stand up for him, Ben would say *It's okay, Maggie*, and that made it worse for me.

I remembered the summer days spent in a cave where people once lived in darkness, a place where he could not be seen by anyone, not even himself.

Now my brother was on the phone, his voice crossing two time zones.

"We need to talk about Daddy," Ben said.

"Did he tell you I'd been up there?"

"Yes, but he didn't say a lot except you only stayed one night."

"So he didn't tell you about our little row."

The line was silent for a few moments.

"Can't you just let it go, Maggie?" Ben said, his voice almost a whisper.

"Why just me? He can't let go of things either."

"He's dying," Ben said.

I thought of Ben's hand holding the phone against his ear, his right hand pressed against his scarred cheek. My brother said he was happy now and I believed him, because despite everything that had happened, happiness and forgiveness were his natural states of being. He had a wife and baby and was finishing up a four-year hitch in the military. More cosmetic surgery had been done once he joined the army, and the scars were less visible. You had to look carefully now to realize he'd been scarred not by acne but by boiling liquid.

"Are you listening to me, Maggie?" Ben asked.

"Yes. But it's not just about him and me. It's about how he treated you."

"He was angry at himself, frustrated he couldn't do anything to make it better for me."

"So if you can't make something better you make it worse."

"We've been over this before. He couldn't help it. I knew that even as a kid, Maggie. I think you did too."

"He could help it," I said. "He could have thought less about his own feelings and more about yours. It was the same with Momma's cancer."

"Sometimes you have to forgive people," Ben said.

"Maybe I'm not like you," I said. "Maybe I'm not as good a person as you are."

"It's not about being good or bad," Ben said. "It's about being afraid of what you'll feel if you can't feel hurt and anger."

"I thought your night classes were in business, little brother, not psychology."

For a few moments we listened to a silence that stretched across a continent.

"So why did you really call?"

"I talked to Dr. Rogers yesterday," Ben said. "He thinks

Daddy will need the most help in the fall. I'll be out of the army at the end of October. I was supposed to take a job here with an insurance company. I talked to them, and they can hold the position until January. Lee Ann will stay here with the baby while I stay with Daddy. But he may live longer than the doctors think or get sicker sooner."

"And if that happens you want me to take care of him."

"Yes. Aunt Margaret's too old to do it by herself."

"And if I don't?"

"He'll be put in the hospital or a nursing home. You know he doesn't want that. He's the same as Momma."

"I can't do it."

"Can't or won't? . . . Well?" Ben asked when I didn't reply.

"It's late here, Ben," I said, "and I have a full day tomorrow. Tell Lee Ann hello for me."

The afternoon Luke had first visited the house, Daddy and I wounded each other as best we could while Momma lay dying in the next room. We'd given voice to every spiteful, hateful thought our hearts had held for each other. Had used up years of them in those few minutes.

Yet our hearts weren't empty. It was as if we had miscalculated how much we could say to each other and still have enough resentment left to cover what ·lay deepest, what could only be expressed with words of reconciliation and forgiveness—words that acknowledged we were bonded by blood and family and, as much as we might wish otherwise, even love. Words so frightening we sealed our mouths tight, risked not a syllable of that language. Because we both realized once you open your mouth to speak such words you open your heart too. You open it wide as a barn door and you take off the hinges and then anything could get out or in, and what can be more frightening than that?

Ben had been the same way. All those years he'd never once given voice to the pain he felt, whether it was pain from another skin graft or from a classmate's cruelty. Maybe that was what happened when people grew up in a place where mountains shut them in, kept everything turned inward, buffered them from everything else. How long did it take before that landscape became internalized, was passed down generation to generation like blood type or eye color?

So we spoke only the words we felt comfortable with that Sunday afternoon, and in the days and months that followed as well, until now nine years had passed and any other language had become hopelessly foreign, untranslatable.

CHAPTER 7

I went straight to the statehouse Tuesday morning to photograph the latest protest against the Confederate flag flying on capitol grounds. When I got back to the office, thirty e-mails awaited me. The first was from Allen, who was in Cheraw. He'd driven there to do a story about a woman who claimed to be Elvis Presley and Marilyn Monroe's love child.

I was glad he was doing the story. A good dose of southern zaniness offered him a much-needed reprieve from the story he'd just written, the story he would resume on Friday when we returned to Oconee County for the second meeting.

"I'll be back in Columbia by noon Friday, so let's plan on leaving by two o'clock," Allen's e-mail said, "unless this woman suddenly produces the birth certificate for Elvilyn

Presley she claims is hidden in the Memphis courthouse vault. If that happens I may be a little late."

I clicked to the other messages, most of which congratulated me on the photograph, including one from an editor at the *Charlotte Observer* asking if I'd send a résumé her way. I read the e-mail from lmiller@Tamassee.org last. There was no subject or greeting.

"I expected what Hemphill would do, but you disappoint me. You understand what's at stake up here. Or maybe I should say you once did. A lot of people have devoted a significant part of their lives to saving the Tamassee. You have betrayed every one of those people. It's the only free-flowing river left in this state. Is it too much to ask that one river in South Carolina not be turned into a lake or open sewer? Just one, Maggie, one river left alone? Is that so radical, so uncompromising?"

I read the message again. Blunt and to the point, classic Luke. In spite of myself, I smiled, thinking back to the first time I found myself on the receiving end of Luke's directness. It was the summer after my sophomore year at Clemson. We'd been at Mama Tilson's because Momma hadn't felt up to cooking. Having come straight from my summer job potting plants at Ellis Gillespie's nursery, I'd washed my face and hands in the bathroom, but black dirt was wedged under my nails and stained my T-shirt and jeans.

That's the troublemaker Harley beat up, Daddy had said, nodding toward the counter where a man was sitting down. *I'd have thought him to have the sense to tuck tail and leave after a whipping like that.* The man's face was scabbed and bruised.

Stitches stubbled a black crescent on his chin. So that's Luke Miller, I'd thought, because I'd heard about him, not just from Daddy but other people such as Billy, who admired him. He seemed not to care that several people now glared at him, including my father. And that impressed me, his not giving a damn, not being afraid Harley or one of his cronies might be around.

When we finished eating I went to the bathroom while the rest of the family went on outside. As I passed the counter I stopped and told Luke how much I admired his attempts to protect the Tamassee. He'd replied brusquely, telling me admiration didn't do a damn thing for the river, that if I wanted to do something that did matter I should come to the community center tomorrow at ten and help address envelopes.

Billy and a few other locals came that Saturday, as did some middle-aged and elderly people from as far away as Columbia and Atlanta. And of course the river rats, not wearing bright-colored river shorts and polypro shirts and Tevas as they would years later but cut-off jeans and tank tops and tennis shoes. The men wore their hair long and attempted beards with varying degrees of success. The women wore their hair long as well. They didn't wear bras and, like the men, were tanned and muscled from long days paddling the river. Luke moved among us, distributing address lists, envelopes, and stamps.

They had all heard what had happened, but it was obvious a number of people inside the community center hadn't seen Luke since Harley Winchester had beaten him up. They studied his battered face, the way his cracked rib made his breathing shallow and quick, like an animal panting. But what struck me was that, unlike my father, the people who'd gathered that Saturday morning weren't surprised he was there. One of the river rats said aloud what Luke's damaged body proved—that nothing short of being killed would keep Luke from trying to save the Tamassee.

I lifted my eyes from the computer screen. There was no reason to reply to Luke's message. I hit the delete button and closed the program.

I WAS EATING THE GRANOLA BAR THAT WOULD BE MY LUNCH when Lee Gervais walked over, the front page in his hand. My photograph filled the bottom third right corner, the first six paragraphs of Allen's story on the left. *A father's grief*, the photo caption read. FATHER FIGHTS RIVER AND LAW TO BRING DAUGHTER HOME headlined the article.

Lee folded the paper so it looked like a baton used in a track meet. He held it in his right hand and shook it for emphasis.

"We've already gotten more response on this than anything in months, and I mean anything, even the damn flag controversy. Senator Jenkins's office called this morning. They wanted it made clear the senator would do everything possible to help Kowalsky get his daughter back. Reuters just called too. They're picking this up, photograph and article both."

Lee grinned.

"You're in high cotton, girl."

"Am I?"

"Sure, it's a good bet other places will pick that photo up as well, maybe even a magazine or two."

"I'm not sure how that works. I've never had to worry about it before."

"At the least you'll get a photo credit," Lee said. "Someone like *Newsweek* picks it up you'll get a couple hundred bucks. It could mean a raise too."

"Does this mean I can get that Volvo I've been wanting all my life?"

"Well, if not that, at least a new muffler for your Escort." Lee nodded at the paper. "Hudson's a happy man. He finally got Hemphill to write something of consequence. This is the best thing that could happen for everyone involved."

DOGWOOD BLOSSOMS NO LONGER BRIGHTENED THE WOODS AS we drove up Stumphouse Mountain. Instead, the oval leaves blended with the surrounding hardwoods. Sarvis bloomed by the road, interspersed with purple and yellow beardtongue and ragwort. A fresh-picked vase of birdfoot violets lay next to one of the crosses.

I yawned, loud enough that Allen looked over at me. I had slept only a few hours the night before. Three A.M. is the hour of doubt, and Luke's e-mail seemed engraved in my mind. Except for our stop at a McDonald's near Greenville, my eyes had been closed most of the trip.

"Sorry to nap the whole way," I said. "I didn't get a lot of sleep last night."

"Me either," Allen said. "Kowalsky called at eleven. Somehow he managed to track me to Aiken. He's already gotten phone calls of support from Senator Jenkins and the governor, and his congressman is flying down from Washington to be at the meeting. Jenkins and the governor are sending some of their staff people to represent them at the meeting as well."

Allen smiled.

"Kowalsky said the piece has made people realize what's really going on up there, but we can't let up the pressure on the other side."

"We?" I asked. "So we're on Kowalsky's side?"

"Those are Kowalsky's words, not mine. I tried to be fair in that article. I didn't demonize Luke or take cheap shots at the search and rescue squad or Forest Service. Is it wrong to show some sympathy for the man?"

For the first time since I'd known him, I heard anger in Allen's voice, anger directed at me.

"No, not at all," I said.

"I'm going up there to cover a story to its conclusion, not to be somebody's mouthpiece. But yes, if I have to choose a side, I'm on Kowalsky's."

"I'm sorry," I said, touching his wrist with my hand. "I wasn't criticizing you."

Allen's voice softened.

"I'm just a little defensive today. Some woman left a message on my answering machine last night. She told me I was trying to single-handedly destroy the Tamassee River, and the only reason was because I couldn't get past my own daughter's death."

"That was a cruel thing to say."

"But maybe it's true. I said much the same thing to you the other night."

We were near the top of Stumphouse now, nearly 2,500 feet above sea level. In the woods a few dogwood blossoms lingered like stars in a dawn sky.

"I've got one more question for you," I said.

Allen glanced at me warily. "Let's hear it," he said.

"Does Elvilyn take after her dad or her mom?"

"Definitely her mom," Allen said. "She has the same peroxide-blond hair."

"What further proof does anyone need?"

"I agree," Allen said. "Seeing is believing." He freed his wrist from my hand to check his watch. "It's a good thing we made that pit stop to eat. We barely have enough time to check in before heading to the meeting."

We passed the Laurel Mist development sign. The bullet holes in the fawn had been caulked.

"I've got a question for you," Allen said. "Why, if you majored in English, do you use a camera instead of a word processor? I mean, was it an aesthetic or philosophical choice?"

"More a wanting-to-be-employed choice, at least at first," I said. "My first boss said my writing was too florid, that if I was going to imitate a writer it should be Hemingway, not Faulkner. He had a point. I'd spend three paragraphs describing the inside of the Moose Lodge when he wanted two hundred words on their latest membership drive."

"So you don't necessarily view us wordsmiths as inferior."

"Not at all," I said. "You're the one making judgments in that department."

Allen groaned. "As I've said before, that was a youthful indiscretion. I'll admit right here and now that there have been times when pictures were truer than words. Am I going to have to sign a blood oath to convince you?"

"No, just a specific example."

"The Civil War. You go back and read first-person newspaper accounts, and you'd think they'd been out there playing baseball four years. It's Matthew Brady's photographs that capture what really happened."

"Like the photo of the dead rebel sharpshooter at Gettysburg?"

"Exactly," Allen said.

"That photograph was staged."

"What do you mean?"

"That man died in a field. They moved his body to the sniper's perch. Even the gun doesn't fit. It's an infantryman's rifle, not a sharpshooter's."

"I never knew that," Allen said. "But you could still argue it's true to the horror of war, truer than those 'factual' accounts of correspondents. Brady captured the crucial truth. The soldier was dead, and he'd died young and violently. Brady didn't arrange that."

"And you yourself would buy that argument?"

"Yes," Allen said, as we passed Billy's store. "Wouldn't you?"

"I think so," I said.

THIRTY MINUTES BEFORE THE SECOND PUBLIC HEARING BEGAN, the last chair in the community center had filled. Cameramen from Charlotte and Columbia and Atlanta TV stations staked out the far corners. Three dozen journalists held note pads and tape recorders in their laps and hands, almost as many photographers interspersed among them. A long table had been placed beside the lectern, metal folding chairs behind it. The two placards on the table said WALTER PHILLIPS, DISTRICT RANGER and DANIEL LUCKADOO, STATE SUPERVISOR OF FORESTS.

Phillips was standing off to the side talking to Myra Burrell. Lee hadn't been interested in any shots of Phillips, but I had developed them anyway, then arranged the photos across a desk as though a police line-up. *Will the real Walter Phillips please step forward*, I told the photographs. And one of them, the one with the widest perspective, seemed to.

It was the hands, the way he had balled them into fists, like a man ready and willing to stand and fight if pushed far enough. But how far was far enough? As I watched Phillips talk to Myra Burrell I wondered if tonight I'd find out.

At five minutes to seven, Phillips and Luckadoo sat down behind the placards. Myra Burrell filled the third chair.

The last time I'd seen Daniel Luckadoo had been seven years ago at a Forest Watch ceremony. He was grayer now and near retirement. It was obvious from his demeanor that Luckadoo wished he was retired right now, was not here but sitting instead on a screened-in porch sipping an after-dinner drink. But before he could get his gold watch and lake house rocking chair he'd have to drive up here to play Solomon.

I turned to Allen. "So how soon after the meeting does Luckadoo make the decision?"

"Kowalsky said tomorrow morning."

"What do you think he'll do?"

"Allow it. He's getting a lot of political pressure to go that way, from the governor on down. Luckadoo has the look of a man who understands the good-old-boy system."

I nodded. Luckadoo had been appointed Supervisor of Forests by a governor who wouldn't have cared if every tree in the state had been cut down. Over the years Luckadoo's actions, especially in regard to clear-cutting, made it evident he shared the governor's philosophy.

Allen nodded toward the front row where Kowalsky sat. Brennon sat on one side of Kowalsky, talking to a man wearing the only suit and tie in the building. On the other side of Kowalsky was a woman I'd never seen before.

"They think it's a done deal. Brennon has already flown the dam down here, as well as the men and materials to put it up. All that does is put more pressure on Luckadoo."

"True," I said, looking over to the corner where Sheriff Cantrell and Hubert McClure stood. "But somebody must have thought this wasn't going to be smooth sailing, else the law wouldn't be here."

I felt a hand on my shoulder, a firm hand.

"Proud of what you've wrought, Maggie?" Luke asked.

"I can't help it that girl is in the river," I said, my voice more defensive than I'd have liked.

"No," Luke said, "but you've given them cause to get her out."

Luke turned away before I could reply.

People leaned against walls and sat in the aisles while others huddled at the door. My photograph had helped fill this room. I watched Luke walk toward the front where Carolyn had saved him a seat.

I'M STARTING TO THINK MAGGIE IS MORE THAN A DILETTANTE, Luke had said in this same room eight years earlier. That morning was the fourth Saturday in a row I'd shown up, and Luke's words served as confirmation not only to me but to all the others that I was truly one of them.

It wasn't just my desire to help save the river that had brought me back to the community center each Saturday. Luke Miller was a handsome man, a fact I wasn't alone in noticing. I began to dress like the others, not just the T-shirt and cut-off jeans but the pigtails and face free of makeup. Before Daddy stopped letting me drive the truck I'd take my bra off somewhere between the house and the community center and stuff it in the dash.

The weekend before I went back to Clemson, Luke asked me if I wanted to go canoeing. He knew every current, every depth, every wood snag and rock. He knew where to enter each sluice. The river rats had told me Luke sometimes kay-aked the river at night, and I'd assumed they meant clear nights with a waxing moon and plenty of stars. But as we made our way downstream that last Sunday in August I realized he wouldn't need light. He could navigate the river blind.

We stopped and ate our lunch. After we finished, Luke

took my hand and we walked up the bank of Lindsey Creek to where a waterfall spilled into a pool wide and deep as a hay wagon. Luke reached into a gap behind the waterfall and lifted out a battered tin dipper. He filled it with water and drank.

"Aren't you afraid you'll get sick?" I asked.

"No. This water's from three springs, and every one of them is on forest land. It's the purest water in the state." Luke filled the dipper again and held it out to out me. "As the poet said, 'Drink and be whole again beyond confusion.' "

I drank water so cold my teeth ached, and then we sat on the bank's plush, cool moss.

"This is my favorite place in the whole watershed," Luke said. "Sometimes I'll spend most of an afternoon here."

"Are you usually alone?" I asked.

"Usually," Luke replied.

He had let go of my hand when we sat down and hadn't reached for it again. He sat with his legs tucked to his chest. I leaned back on my elbows, my left hand palm up and close to his hip. Luke pointed to a shiny-green plant on the other side of the pool.

"You know that one?"

Mountain laurel surrounded the plant, and I thought it might be a sprout. But I didn't want to venture a guess and sound stupid if I were wrong.

"No," I said.

"Oconee Bell," Luke said, taking my hand. "When they built Jocassee Reservoir they destroyed two-thirds of the

Oconee Bells in the world. Think about that. In the world."

I moved closer to him. "The ones here should be safe at least," I said, because in mid-August the Tamassee's Wild and Scenic status had been approved by the House. We were careful not to be overconfident so we kept forwarding the petitions and letters, but it looked more and more certain the Senate would vote our way.

My left hand lifted Luke's right. I raised his hand to my mouth and kissed it.

"So are you on the pill?" he asked.

"No," I said, trying not to sound stunned by the question.

"I've got a rubber in my dry pack."

"I don't think," I said, and stopped there. I tried again. "I can't, I haven't."

Luke laughed.

"You surprise me, Maggie Glenn. I figured one of those college boys at Clemson would have talked you into his dorm-room bed by now. One probably has, but you're one of those 'technical virgins,' right?"

I was glad our hands concealed much of my face because I knew it burned red, not so much from the wording as from the comment's truth. It was as if he'd somehow been witness to those moments of groping, starting, and stopping in dorm rooms and backseats of cars. Despite two years at Clemson, I still adhered to the rules of Oconee County females, a code abandoned in the sixties by most of the United States but still practiced and enforced in much of the rural South. On the surface it was simple: A woman was supposed to stay a virgin until married, but what exactly constituted virginity, that murky area between heavy petting and going all the way, was a question of byzantine complexity.

But Luke wasn't interested in testing the limits of such a code. He stood, pulling me up as well. He freed his hand from mine.

"Let me know if you change your mind."

His tone was matter-of-fact, in a way almost good-humored, the opposite of the exasperation I'd encountered in all of my other sexual skirmishes. This is what it's like to deal with a man instead of a boy, I told myself. Which only showed how much of a girl I still was.

Four weeks passed before I called Luke from Clemson and told him I wanted to canoe the Tamassee again. He knew my meaning.

"It'll have to be this weekend," Luke said. "Next week I'm off to Florida to help a friend get Wild and Scenic status for the Suwannee. She helped with the Tamassee so I owe her."

We launched early on a Saturday morning. Fog rose off the river and got tangled in the trees lining the banks. It was still late summer in Clemson, but here fall had already begun. Leaves were turning and the air was so cool we'd paddled a half mile before I took off my sweatshirt.

The fog finally thinned and the sun broke through. When it did we were in a section where stands of poplar trees lined both shores. As the last smudges of fog evaporated, the yellow sun-struck poplar leaves brightened like lamp wicks being turned up. The air felt charged and alive, like when lightning breaks the sky before rain. Though we were in slow water, the river's pulse seemed to quicken. Everything, including Luke and me, shimmered in a golden light. For the first time in my life I saw the river the way I believed Luke saw it.

A Church of God preacher in Mountain View had denounced us as "false prophets" who worshiped nature, not God, as though one were not part of the other. At the community center we'd kidded ourselves about being religious zealots, the males giving each other nicknames that began with the word saint, we females adding Magdalene to our first names.

But Luke had never joined in the joking. On that September morning I understood his seriousness, that what we were trying to save *was* holy, for I was not just in the presence of something sacred and eternal but for a few seconds inside it. "Spots of time" was the phrase Wordsworth used for such moments, but the poet's words were no better than mine because what I felt was beyond any words that had ever been used before. You needed a new language, as members of the church I'd grown up in sometimes did when they'd been possessed by the Holy Ghost and spoken in tongues. They had writhed in the pews and aisles, their bodies contorted as though each word had to be wrenched physically free from its place in the heart. But even in those moments no one knew what they were saying, not even themselves.

We paddled on downstream. The sky widened blue above the gorge, the sun warming the river enough that light hatches of dun-colored caddis flies dimpled some pools.

"So how long will you be in Florida?" I asked.

"Probably until the rafting season starts back up."

"I didn't know you'd be gone that long," I said, and must have sounded wistful because Luke laughed.

"You sound like you're going to miss me, Maggie."

"I will," I said.

"Well, you'll have plenty of time to be around me next summer. I talked to Earl Wilkinson, and he said it's okay if you work with us as a photographer come May. You won't get rich, but you'll make as much as you would potting plants. That is, if you want the job."

"Yes," I said. "I want it."

"Good," Luke said. "I'll tell him."

We didn't speak again until we came to where Lindsey Creek entered the Tamassee. As we got out of the canoe, I lifted Luke's dry pack from the bow and brought it with us.

WALTER PHILLIPS STEPPED TO THE PODIUM AT SEVEN SHARP. HE introduced Luckadoo and set the ground rules: five minutes a person, and anyone who caused a disturbance would not only be thrown out but also arrested.

Kowalsky again spoke first, covering much the same terrain as at the first meeting, and just as abrasively, before introducing the man in the suit as his congressman. The congressman shook Kowalsky's hand and then spoke briefly, his main point being that he represented not just himself and the Kowalsky family but all of the people of Minnesota in urging that the dam be allowed. After the congressman finished, Senator Jenkins's aide expressed the senator's sympathy for the Kowalskys as well as his full support in helping recover their daughter's body. The governor's representative echoed their sentiments. Brennon spoke as well, emphasizing the minimal environmental impact.

Then Luke had his turn, again reading excerpts from the Wild and Scenic Rivers legislation. He didn't look at Kowalsky or Phillips or anyone in the audience. When Luke looked up from the papers he read, his eyes were on Luckadoo. But Luckadoo's eyes did not leave the watch he'd placed on the table, and though Luckadoo had a pen in his hand, he did not write down a word as Luke made his argument.

"Your five minutes are up," Luckadoo announced, looking at Luke for the first time since he'd begun speaking.

Billy was in the row in front of me. He turned around. "Luckadoo didn't even pretend to listen," Billy said. "This isn't looking good at all."

The only group of people who hadn't spoken were the locals, and none of them did until the meeting was almost over.

I hadn't seen my father until he rose, slowly, unsteadily, from his chair in the second row, his hand grasping the shoulder of the man who sat beside him. I couldn't see his face but his hair was washed and combed. He wore the one suit he owned.

"He shouldn't be here," I said. "He's too sick."

"Who?" Allen asked.

"My father."

Daddy lifted a handkerchief from his back pocket and

wiped his mouth. He had once been able to fill an entire barn loft with square-baled hay in a single afternoon, a man strong enough to carry hundred-pound fertilizer sacks two at a time, but now the effort of rising from a chair winded him. I didn't want to feel sorry for him, but I couldn't look away.

"My nephew Joel ought to be saying this, but he's washed his hands of this mess," Daddy said, looking around the room as he spoke, "so I'll say it for him. If this is a matter of drilling a few holes in the riverbed, that's the thing that ought to be done. But this is a safety issue as well. I've lived on this river sixty-six years. I know the river and Joel knows it and the rest of that search-and-rescue squad knows it. One summer a few years back nine people drowned in the Tamassee. Just in that one summer. It got so bad they stretched a big net under Holder Bridge to catch the bodies."

Daddy paused to wipe the spittle from his mouth again. He turned in my direction and I saw he wore his white shirt and a tie as well as the suit. I suddenly realized that the next time he'd be wearing these clothes he might well be in his casket. I wondered if he recognized the same thing.

"Those boys know what they're doing, and they've done all they could to get that body out. Anybody who says otherwise is wrong."

He paused again.

"We all make mistakes, and sometimes we pay a high price for them. That girl made a mistake when she tried to cross that river, she paid the highest price of all. She didn't know how dangerous that river was, but you've all been told now.

You just be sure that dam works, Mr. Brennon, because that river isn't something to trifle with."

The man beside Daddy helped him sit back down.

"Is that it?" Luckadoo asked, his eyes sweeping the room. "If so, I'm going to give the last five minutes to Ruth Kowalsky's mother."

Mrs. Kowalsky stepped up to the lectern. She wore a black dress that reached closer to her ankles than her knees, and I wondered if like my father she also wore funeral clothes, not for herself but for her daughter.

She was a tall slim woman, a woman who had retained her beauty into middle age, conceding only a few wrinkles around the eyes and mouth. Her hair was frosted blond, cut short and stylishly by someone very talented and no doubt very expensive. But her beauty seemed fragile as an eggshell. You could tell something had broken inside her in the halting way she walked to the lectern.

"Oh, shit," one of the river rats sitting with Luke said. He hadn't spoken loudly, but the room was so still his words carried like a shout.

"My name is Ellen Kowalsky, and I'm Ruth's mother," she began. "My husband didn't want me to come tonight. But I had to. You didn't know Ruth, but I'm going to tell you about her, because maybe if I can give you some sense of what she was like, you will understand why it's so important to us to take her home, to give her a proper burial."

Ellen Kowalsky spoke slowly, her words carefully enunciated, making each word seem tentative, difficult. She did not look at us but above and past us. Her eyes were fixed on the back wall as though she were scaling it, each word she spoke another piton.

She'll never make it through this, I said to myself, because her eyes already glistened with tears. I thought of her diving into the pool below Wolf Cliff Falls, hands searching for her daughter as she moved along the bottom until she'd had to surface. What had she thought or said to her husband as he restrained her from entering the pool a third time? Had she begged him to let her go, tried to break free from his grasp?

I tried to imagine what it would be like to watch your child being swept away. How many nights would you wake in the dark, gasping for breath, as you thought of her trying to breathe? How often would you wonder if you'd only gone to Grandfather Mountain or Asheville your daughter would be alive now?

No, I couldn't imagine what those moments had been like for Ellen Kowalsky, but as I glanced over at Allen's face I knew he could, that there were times he thought about what his life would be like now if he'd taken an earlier flight, or a later one, or told his wife he'd take a taxi home or decided, as she'd evidently wished, not to go to Kosovo at all.

Walter Phillips got up from his chair, as if to offer his seat to Ellen Kowalsky.

"You don't have to do this, Ellen," Herb Kowalsky said, a tenderness in his voice I'd not heard before. That tenderness surprised me and, I suspected, a number of other people in the room. But maybe not his wife. I wondered if I had made some judgments about Herb Kowalsky that were a little too easy and convenient. Yet even as I thought this another part of me remembered the scorn in his voice when he'd spoken of hillbillies.

"Yes, I do," Ellen Kowalsky replied, glancing back at her husband as she spoke. She blinked quickly and for a few moments stared at the back wall again, securing her hold before continuing. She took a deep breath and lowered her eyes so she might see ours.

"I could tell you Ruth was the perfect child, that she never gave her father or me any trouble and was always good to her brother."

A woman on the second row began to cry, loud enough to make Ellen Kowalsky pause and raise her eyes to the back wall again.

"But you'd know that couldn't be true of any child, so I'll tell what's true, that there were times Ruth tried our patience, times we had to punish her, times she disappointed us."

The *Atlanta Constitution*'s photographer took a photo. Several people turned and glared at him. Neither he nor anyone else took another one.

"In other words, she was like anybody else's child. But there were times we were short-tempered with her when we shouldn't have been and times we didn't give her as much attention and love as we could have. Any parent in this room knows how that can happen. We get so caught up in our own lives we forget that nothing's more important than our children. We always say we'll make it up to them tomorrow or this weekend or on a birthday or Christmas. We assume that tomorrow or that birthday is going to come."

Ellen Kowalsky had used up her allotted time, but no one in the room was going to tell her that. Her voice softened even more, almost a whisper now, as if she were in a confessional booth instead of a rural community center.

"But sometimes that day doesn't come, and the things you meant to do or say can't be said or done because the child is no longer there. The vacation was my idea. It seemed like we hadn't been seeing each other much, not even eating meals at the same time. I thought a few days together would bring us closer as a family. And it had. We'd had two good days together, until we came here."

Ellen Kowalsky paused for a few moments. The room was so quiet I could hear crickets chirping outside the open windows. Suddenly I realized Ellen Kowalsky wasn't looking at the back wall. She was looking *through* it, past the bridge and Bobcat Rock, all the way to that undercut inside Wolf Cliff Falls.

"I can only do one more thing for Ruth, and that is to get her out of the river, because it's not just her body down there but her soul. That's what my church has said for hundreds of years—that a person is in purgatory until the body is given Last Rites. My husband, even my priest, say they don't believe that."

Ellen Kowalsky lowered her eyes and looked straight at us.

"But what if they're wrong?"

No one in the room was ready for that statement. The reporters and other outsiders might have written off Ellen Kowalsky's concern as a bizarre symptom of her grief, but I knew many of the locals, though low-church Protestants, would not dismiss her fear or its premise.

Ellen Kowalsky continued to look at us as she spoke.

"I've already tried to bring Ruth out of that place, and I couldn't do it, at least not by myself. I need the help of Mr. Brennon and his dam. And I need the Forest Service and the rest of the people in this room to support Mr. Brennon. It's the last thing I can do," she said, her voice starting to falter. "It's too late for anything else."

At that moment not even the most cynical person in the room could have doubted that the loss of her child had broken Ellen Kowalsky, and that she would not begin to heal until her child was buried in earth, not water.

Brennon stood by the chair Ellen Kowalsky sat in. He leaned toward her, his hand on her shoulder. He spoke, and she nodded. Brennon's facial expression made clear his concern about recovering Ruth was now emotional as well as professional.

Billy turned to me and shook his head. "It's a done deal," he said.

Luke knew as well as Billy that he had lost. What restraint he'd had so far disappeared. As soon as Daniel Luckadoo said the meeting was adjourned Luke started to the front, weaving through the people who filled the aisle.

"It's federal law, Luckadoo," he shouted. "Federal law. It's not something you or anybody else decides. It's been decided, and if you allow this dam you're breaking the law and you know it."

Sheriff Cantrell and Hubert McClure grabbed Luke by the arms before he could say anything else. They shoved him through the crowd and out the door. People soon began to follow them out.

I left Allen and made my way to the second row of chairs where Daddy still sat.

"You shouldn't have come," I said.

Daddy looked up at me.

"I figured no one else would say some things that needed to be said. It turned out I was right."

"Who brought you?" I asked, because Daddy hadn't been sitting with anyone I knew.

"Joel dropped me off. He wouldn't come in though."

"When's he coming back to get you?"

"I don't know that he will. I figured to get a ride with someone heading out that way."

I looked around the room. Billy was gone as well as anyone else who might be driving down Damascus Church Road.

"Did Joel say he'd be at home?" I asked.

"He didn't say."

I looked up front. Myra Burrell had not left, but she lived back toward the river.

"Let me get the car keys," I said.

"You don't have to take me," Daddy said, the stubbornness in his voice pricking like a briar.

I walked up to the podium where Allen had joined the circle of reporters around Brennon and Kowalsky.

"I need the car keys so I can take my father home," I told him.

Allen fished the keys from his front pocket. "You want me to go with you?"

"No," I said. "It's not far. I'll be back in fifteen minutes."

"I would like to meet him," Allen said.

"Some other time," I said, and walked out to the parking lot where Daddy waited.

The sun was settling into the trees now, and shadows unfurled up mountainsides. Across the road in Herb Greene's pasture, cows clumped together under trees. Daddy didn't see them. If he had he'd have said it was a sure sign of coming rain.

"You ought to turn on your headlights," Daddy said, as I pulled out of the parking lot.

"I know how to drive," I said, then turned on the headlights anyway. It was simpler to do so.

"It seems I can't ever say the right thing to you," he said, his words low, too low to tell which of us he felt was responsible for that.

We passed Billy's store. Billy and Wanda sat on the porch while their boys kicked a ball in the parking lot.

Daddy shifted in his seat. I looked at the road but I knew his eyes were on me.

"There's things I got to say to you," he said.

It seemed unlikely, but I wondered if he'd planned on me driving him home. Done it just to get me in a place where I had to hear him out. Daddy's voice trembled when he spoke.

"There ain't a day goes by I don't think about me leaving you and Ben alone. I forgot all about those beans on the stove. I'd have never went to the store if I hadn't."

"I don't want to hear this," I said.

"Your Momma forgave me. Your brother, the one with the most right to be hard-hearted, he forgave me. But you ain't and maybe God ain't either. You know what it says in Matthew, Maggie. You ain't forgot all your Bible yet, have you? 'But whosoever shall hurt one of these little ones which believe in me, it were better for him that a millstone were hanged about his neck, and that he were drowned in the depth of the sea.' "

I turned onto Damascus Church Road, but the house was still a mile away. I pressed the radio's ON-OFF button, but I'd forgotten how few stations reached this deep into the mountains. Allen had the radio on the AM band. All I got was static.

"Do you know how many times that verse jabbed barb-deep in my heart? I know what I done," Daddy said, his voice trembling, "and not just to Ben but to you."

How damn convenient this is, I thought. You wait till you're dying and make this dramatic confession and everything's set straight, everything's forgiven, a perfect Hollywood ending.

"I blame myself and always have," Daddy said.

Don't let him pull you into this, I'd been telling myself the last few minutes, but the self-pity in his voice made me speak.

"Then why did you treat Ben like it was his fault?" I said. "Why didn't you ever tell me that I shouldn't blame myself, that it was your fault, not mine? It mattered then."

I crossed over Licklog Creek and then up the last rise. I drove up to the house and put the car in park but did not turn off the engine.

"Why can't it matter now?" Daddy asked.

Because I don't want to let you off that easy, I thought. Because you're the only one left to blame.

"I've got to go," I said.

Daddy got out of the car and closed the door. I watched him slowly climb the steps, his hand gripping the rail. Please don't look back at me, I thought, and he didn't.

I drove back to the community center, the place where two decades earlier the pig picking had been held to help my family pay Ben's hospital bills. Neighbors and friends had brought yellowware filled with cole slaw and baked beans and potato salad, gallon jars of sweet tea and homemade ice cream still in the churns. The women covered tables with food and drinks while Daddy and the other men huddled out back with Lou Henson as he basted the pig with a paintbrush.

I'd been inside with Aunt Margaret and the other women. They made a fuss over me, telling me how pretty I was and how much I'd grown. They were good women and they meant well, but it somehow made it all worse, being treated like I'd just been baptized or had a birthday and Ben still in the burn center in Columbia with only Momma there with him. I made my way out the back door, walking as fast as I could down the path to the creek, my hand over my nose and mouth to block out the smell of burning pig.

I sat by myself on the bank until Aunt Margaret came. Though she wore a dress she sat down beside me. "I know this is a hard time for you, girl," Aunt Margaret had said. "But it's going to get better." It could have been five minutes or it could have been thirty, but Daddy came down to the creek as well. He carried two paper plates sagging with food. He handed us the plates and plastic forks and napkins, then went back to get our tea. He sat down beside me on the bank. "I reckon we've had about as much kindness as we can stand," he'd said, as his left hand settled awkwardly on my shoulder.

It was not a convenient memory, because I couldn't frame it neatly into the black-and-white photograph I'd made of my past.

WHEN I ENTERED THE COMMUNITY CENTER, ALLEN AND ONE other reporter remained with Luckadoo, Phillips, and the Kowalskys. A few river rats lingered at the back, looking lost without Luke.

"You all right?" Allen asked, as we drove back to the motel. "You looked upset when you first came back."

"I'm fine now."

"This problem between you and your father, is it something recent?"

"No."

"Want to talk about it?"

"Not tonight. Maybe some other time."

Allen's right hand touched my arm. "We can talk of other things, though. Right?"

"Right," I said.

At the motel Allen parked the car and turned off the ignition. Neither of us reached for the door latch.

"So what other things do you want to talk about tonight?"
I asked.

Allen looked straight at me. "How about that I'm falling in
love with you. That I want to be with you tonight, but I'm
not sure that's what you want."

"It's what I want," I said.

"It's been a year and a half," Allen said. "I'm not sure how
well it will go."

"I think we're after something more significant than a one-
night stand," I said. "Tonight won't decide what happens
between us."

A Chevy Blazer pulled into the lot, and one of the cameramen who'd been at the meeting got out and entered the
lobby. The motel's gaudy neon sign flickered on. For the first
time I could remember, the Tamassee River Motel flashed its
NO VACANCY sign.

As the parking lot filled up around us, the room windows
brightened. Occasionally there was the sound of an ice bucket
being filled, a door being shut. Lightning bugs sparked as they
hovered above grass already dampened with dew. We left the
car and went to our separate rooms.

In the bathroom I found that the onset of love had not
produced any miracles as far as my appearance, so I settled
for what cosmetics could do. Many of the older people in
Tamassee believed mirrors were passageways between the living and the dead, and after funerals every mirror in a house
was veiled so the departed couldn't return. Aunt Margaret had
done the same when Momma died, shrouding each one with
a piece of dark muslin. I wondered what Claire Pritchard-

Hemphill might feel if she watched me prepare myself to make love to her husband. A dim sadness? Or perhaps the dead were beyond such human concerns.

I cut off the light and went into the main room and sat on the bed. When I heard Allen's footsteps I did not wait for a knock before opening the door.

CHAPTER 8

I woke to the sound of rain. Lying in bed I wondered if the Kowalskys and Brennon also heard that rain and understood what it meant.

"Good morning, sleepyhead," Allen said, when I opened my eyes. He nuzzled close to me.

"It's raining," I said, settling my back deeper into Allen's chest.

"Good," Allen whispered, pressing his mouth against my ear. "There's nothing better than being in bed with a woman on a rainy morning."

"It's not good for Brennon or Kowalsky," I said. "If the Tamassee rises over one and a half feet, I doubt they'll be able to put that dam up even if Luckadoo does give them permission."

"Maybe the rain will let up soon."

"Maybe, but it also depends on what it's doing upstream." I looked at the clock on the lamp table. "Almost eight," I said. "What time will they make the announcement?"

"Phillips said between eleven and twelve. We've still got a little while," he said, as I turned to him.

BY THE TIME WE GOT TO THE RANGER STATION, THE RAIN HAD thinned to drizzle. Fog on the Tamassee's surface smoldered like a doused fire. The air was cool, and I was glad I'd packed a sweatshirt. The calendar might say it was May, but it seemed more like October, the kind of morning I'd always enjoyed on the river, because everything, even the water, was always quieter. On those mornings the fog felt like a countercurrent, moving opposite the earth's rotation to hold everything, even time, in abeyance. I hoped, if Mrs. Kowalsky was somehow right, that this was what her daughter's soul now felt. Not fear or loneliness but a sense of being one with something transcendently beautiful.

"Why the wry smile?" Allen asked, taking my hand.

"A realization that at least in spirit I'm still one of Luke's followers."

"He's not the only person who cares about that river," Allen said, and there was irritation in his voice.

I squeezed his hand.

"I know that. I'm just saying that if you spend enough time

on the Tamassee you can't help but believe a lot of what Luke believes."

Allen freed his hand from mine. "But you don't regret taking the photo?" he asked.

A part of me wanted to answer no and leave it at that, because things were going well between us, too well to let something already done create a problem. But I couldn't do that.

"Yes," I said. "I'm afraid I do."

Anger sparked and caught in Allen's eyes. "And I'm responsible for setting up that photograph, right? That's what you said in my office."

"I could have left it in the darkroom. It was my decision to give it to Lee."

I paused as a camera crew from a Greenville TV station passed. Billy walked toward us, saw our faces, and quickly changed direction.

"So even after last night's meeting you still want Ruth Kowalsky's body to stay in that river?"

"No," I said. "I don't want that. But I don't want the river damaged either. Luke's right about what can happen when a precedent is set."

"And you'd feel that way even if it were your child in that river? You're like Luke that way as well?"

"I don't know what I'd feel," I said.

"No, you don't," Allen said. "But Ellen Kowalsky knows. It's not some abstraction she can look at with detachment."

Nor can you, I thought. Maybe none of us can be detached.

"It's done," I said. "I don't want us to fight about this."

"I don't either," Allen said, but his tone wasn't convincing. He nodded toward the front porch of the ranger station, where the Kowalskys stood with Brennon and the congressman. "But I don't understand why you can't feel good if this woman finally has some closure."

"I will," I said. "About that at least."

When Luckadoo and Walters stepped out of the ranger office, Allen and I moved closer, joining a crowd of over a hundred people. Almost everyone who'd been at last night's meeting had come to hear the Forest Service's decision, including the press, which counted among its ranks two camera crews who had not been present at the community center. I did not see the aides to the governor or Senator Jenkins. They knew the outcome and were already headed back to Columbia and Washington.

Luke had come as well, fresh out of the county jail. He stood with the river rats. Sheriff Cantrell and Hubert McClure leaned against the porch's side railing, their eyes steady on them.

Luckadoo took out a pair of black reading glasses and read from a sheet of paper.

"The Forest Service has decided that under the present circumstances a portable, temporary dam built by Brennon Corporation will be allowed at Wolf Cliff Falls on Section Five of the Tamassee River."

Brennon and Kowalsky shook hands as Mrs. Kowalsky hugged the congressman.

"This will never hold up, Luckadoo," Luke shouted, as a woman held a microphone to his face. "I promise you Sierra

Club lawyers will start petitioning the courts on behalf of the Tamassee this very afternoon."

"Are you saying you believe you can still stop this?" the reporter asked.

"We're going to sure as hell try, lady."

Luke turned from the reporter, and when he did he saw me. He shoved through the dispersing crowd until we were face-to-face. His clothes were soaked. Dark crescents lay beneath his eyes.

"Do you think the Kowalskys understand what they're going to find down there after almost five weeks?" he asked me.

"I don't know," I said, and as soon as I spoke realized I'd kept the truth from myself. Because the image I'd been carrying around in my head was of Ruth Kowalsky minutes after she drowned, not weeks. I'd pictured her in some timeless state. Maybe her soul was, but not her body.

"Well, I have a pretty good idea, Maggie," Luke said, "and you do as well."

And I did, because I knew not only what water could do to a body given time but also what crayfish and larvae and fish could do.

The reporter had trailed Luke over to where we stood. She stuck the microphone back in Luke's face.

"Are you saying the body will be damaged?" she asked.

The stupidity of the question seemed to calm Luke for a moment.

"Get your cameraman over here," he told her. "My answer will make a good segment for your evening news."

The reporter motioned for the cameraman. When Luke saw the red recording light come on, he turned to the camera and began to speak.

"I helped bring a college student out of Bear Sluice two summers ago. He'd only been in there five days, not five weeks. We could get to him, but the water was too strong to pull him out by hand. We tied cable around him and used a winch. We gave the winch five turns and an arm and head came flying out and landed on a sandbar. We got the rest of him out one piece at a time."

The reporter's mouth opened as if she were about to gag. She lowered the microphone, her free hand signaling for the cameraman to stop recording.

Luke turned and moved in, his face only inches from mine.

"That kid's parents were there," Luke said. "They saw it all, Maggie."

"I know that," I said.

Luke was so close I could feel his breath when he spoke. "God, I hope this isn't just some twisted way to get back at me for what happened between me and you years ago."

"Don't flatter yourself," I said, meeting Luke's eyes.

"Ease up, Miller," Allen said, stepping closer to fill the void left by the reporter.

Luke turned to Allen. Eighteen hours of frustration showed on his face.

"A friend of mine sent me information about you she found on the Internet. Information about your wife and daughter. I could tell you what I think your part in this is really about."

Sheriff Cantrell and Hubert McClure were walking rapidly

in our direction. People were clearing a space around us. Carolyn left a bench and walked toward us as well.

Luke turned from Allen and looked at me. "But I won't," Luke said.

Sheriff Cantrell stepped between Luke and Allen.

"What's going on here?" he said.

"Nothing," Luke said. "I'm leaving."

"Good," Sheriff Cantrell said.

"Let's go," Luke said to Carolyn, who stood beside him now.

"One more thing, Miller," Sheriff Cantrell said. "I don't want you or any of your buddies within fifty yards of that dam."

Luke turned away.

"Fifty yards," Sheriff Cantrell reiterated. "If you get any closer to that dam I'll lock you up, and the bond will be a sight higher than five hundred dollars. We clear on that?"

Luke and Carolyn walked across the road to his truck and drove off. I leaned close to Allen.

"You okay?" I asked.

Allen didn't reply.

"Luke was just trying to make you angry."

"No, not angry," Allen said. "He was ready to say some things to hurt me." Allen paused. "But he didn't. If I'd been him I'm not so sure I would have held back."

Allen looked up at the porch where Ellen Kowalsky continued to talk to her congressman. He watched her for almost a minute.

"You want to go back to the motel?" I asked.

"No," Allen said. "I need to ask Brennon a few questions."

"I'll go too," I said. "I might get a good photograph."

Five reporters were already ahead of us. I took out the Nikon and snapped some photos, mainly of Kowalsky, who smiled and patted backs as though he'd finally closed a long negotiated and frustrating business deal. But as soon as that thought came to me I knew I was being unfair. This was probably the first thing he'd had the slightest reason to feel good about in almost a month. I stashed my camera in my backpack and looked at the sky and saw the sun trying to rub through the gray overcast.

"Ask him about the rain," I prodded, as Brennon finished with the reporter in front of us.

Brennon smiled when he saw Allen and me and extended his hand. He was more animated than I'd seen him before.

"Finally some good news, eh?" he said. "And you two had a lot to do with it. That article and photograph made a huge difference, especially with the politicians."

"Good news for you all at least," Allen said.

"Yes," Brennon said. He motioned toward the Kowalskys. "When Herb called two weeks ago and asked me to help I almost said no. But after hearing Ellen last night—well, I'm just glad I'm here."

"What about the rain?" Allen asked.

"One of my people has been keeping tabs. It's not over two feet yet."

I stepped closer.

"You'd go in at two feet?"

"Sure," Brennon said. "We built one last year and the water was two point three."

"But this is white water," I said, trying to keep my voice level.

"Doesn't make any difference. Besides, the river's going down some. It won't be above one point eight before we start."

"And when do you start?" Allen asked.

"Two o'clock this afternoon. My men are waiting at the motel with the equipment. All I have to do now is get in touch with those twins. They're doing the diving. The only problem is, I can't call them because I've forgotten their last name."

"It's Moseley," I said. "Ronny and Randy Moseley."

"Yeah," Brennon said. "That's it."

THERE HAD BEEN A WELL-MAINTAINED CUTBACK TRAIL LEADING to Wolf Cliff Falls, but it no longer existed. The bulldozer we'd passed on the logging road had gouged a new trail—a road-wide, hundred-yard mudslide. Foot traffic made it worse, as people slipped and slid down the ridge, grabbing onto scrub oaks and mountain laurel to keep from tumbling into the river.

"This shouldn't have been allowed," I said to Allen, as we made our way down the ridge. "There will be silt running into the river for years. It will be like a bleeding sore."

"How could they have stopped it?" Allen asked. "The dam had to be brought in."

"They could have gotten it in without using a bulldozer. It's another violation of federal law, and Luckadoo's announcement this morning didn't authorize it."

"An example of Luke's domino theory?" Allen asked.

"I'd say it's no longer a theory. The proof is all around us, isn't it?"

"Yes, it is," Allen said, and his voice was conciliatory. He stopped and lightly gripped my arm so I stopped as well. "Using the bulldozer's wrong," he said. "And I'll say so in my next article."

Allen lowered his voice as two more reporters stumbled past us.

"I don't want this to be a problem between us."

"I don't either," I said, "so we won't let it be."

"Good," Allen said. "When this is over I want to canoe this river. Just you and me. I want to know this watershed the way you do."

Back up the ridge someone cursed. A few moments later a video camera banged down the trail, splitting apart when it hit a river rock.

"One less Channel Seven exclusive," Allen said.

But there were plenty more camera crews and a couple of dozen reporters and photographers. Plenty of gawkers, too, standing and sitting downstream of Wolf Cliff Falls.

Walter Phillips stood at the edge of the pool, a walkie-talkie pressed to his ear. Sheriff Cantrell and Hubert McClure were there as well. Across the river, Luke and his group perched like hawks on a granite outcrop. They were far enough away to keep Sheriff Cantrell happy, though I suspected he would have been even more pleased if they hadn't shown up at all.

More people came down the trail, including Kowalsky and his wife, then Brennon and his crew of eight men who carried the portable dam. Ronny and Randy came with them.

"I'm going to talk with the Kowalskys a minute," Allen said.

I found a place on the bank dried by the sun and sat down. I opened my backpack and made sure the camera equipment and flashlight had not been damaged in the descent.

The sun shone full on Wolf Cliff now, giving the cliff face a silvery sheen. The sky above was blue, though I knew as well as anyone else who lived here how quickly that could change. If that blue sky holds a few hours they'll probably be able to do it, I thought.

Shore rocks dry last week lay partially submerged. Rhododendron leaves that had been untouched now bent with the current. The water itself was clearing but still dingy, like watered-down coffee. Driftwood, twigs, and leaves circled in eddies. I would have guessed two feet above normal.

"Quite a circus, ain't it," Billy said, sitting down beside me.

"Yes, it is," I said, moving over to give him more room. "You think the water will get low enough for them to try?"

"It was two point three at noon. I haven't seen a rafting party yet, so I guess Earl thinks it's still too high. But it is going down. I'd guess an even two now, one point eight at the lowest."

"That's about what I was thinking."

Brennon's men put on bright orange life jackets and clasped

safety belts around their waists. They huddled around Brennon while Ronny and Randy sat together on the bank behind them, caps pulled low over their eyes, their diving equipment beside them.

"Look at that," Billy said, and pointed into the water. A dead raccoon floated downriver, its belly swollen as if pregnant.

"Got swept in, I reckon," Billy said. "They're usually smarter than that."

More people came down the trail.

"Shit," Billy said. "The Forest Service should've put up bleachers and charged admission."

People crowded the bank now, talking excitedly as if waiting for a boat race or athletic contest to begin. Several teenagers took off their shoes and splashed each other in the shallows. A man stood on the rock where I'd photographed Herb Kowalsky. He ate a Hardee's breakfast biscuit as he peered into the water.

I looked upstream and saw Ellen Kowalsky standing on the bank alone. She wore dark slacks and a dress jacket.

Billy looked back up the trail. "Please, Lord," he said, raising his eyes skyward, "let that son of a bitch fall and bust his ass. Let him roll all the way into the river."

I turned and saw Bryan thirty yards up the trail. He wore chinos and a green sports shirt. He also wore a pair of Docksiders, their slick soles offering as much grip on the mud as bald car tires on ice. One hand clutched a limb of mountain laurel. Bryan looked unsure whether to go down or back up.

He moved closer to the plant, using its main stem to secure his right foot. A camera was strapped on his neck and he raised it, photographing the trail and the men installing the dam.

It would set a precedent, Luke had said at the first meeting. Bryan now had proof of that precedent.

Bryan took his final shot and tentatively turned around. He took a step and slipped, righted himself before he fell, and made his way cautiously back up the trail.

"No good can come of those photos," Billy said.

"No," I said. "No good at all."

Allen and Kowalsky stood on the shore edge together, but Kowalsky had turned to watch Brennon's men. Allen faced the river. I stood and raised my camera, focusing in on Allen, bringing his face closer to mine. Allen turned in my direction and when he saw the camera he smiled. I clicked the shutter twice. Maybe I'll have one good memory of this place, I thought, and sat back down.

"Have you heard back from Fish and Wildlife about your photos?" I asked.

"I did," Billy said. "Their mountain lion expert wrote and said they were, in his words, 'very intriguing.' He's in Tennessee, but he said come winter to call him after we get a good snow. He said he'd drive over and we could look for tracks."

"That's exciting," I said. "Your sighting may be verified yet."

"Yes," Billy said. "It would be nice to be proved right. But that's not the best part."

"What's better?"

"Knowing that despite people like Bryan and Luckadoo there's still enough wild acreage left up here to hide a few things."

Billy looked upstream to where Brennon's men worked.

"At least for a little while longer," Billy said.

"Maybe more than a little while," I said. "There are plenty of people who will fight Bryan if he tries to harm this watershed."

"We'll see," Billy said. "But I've got a feeling all this is going to make it a hell of a lot harder."

Across the river Joel emerged from the woods. He was by himself.

"I'm surprised he's come," I said.

"He wants to see himself vindicated," Billy said. "He came in the store yesterday and said he doesn't believe they'll be able to raise one portion of that dam without it being knocked down."

"He might be right," I replied. "Especially if they try today."

Four of Brennon's men hooked ropes onto their belts. Two held jackhammers, two others bracing pins. The men waded into the flat water where Ruth Kowalsky had lost her footing. They moved with care, aiming to plant their feet on sand instead of algae-slick rocks. From the shore Brennon directed them to the places Ronny and Randy had found bedrock and they began to drill.

"Looks like they made up their minds to try," Billy said.

A clattering suddenly rose from above Wolf Cliff, and a helicopter came into view. The machine hovered above the trees like a dragonfly, its shadow falling on the water as a cameraman leaned out to film. The river rats thrust their middle fingers in the air. Several people on the bank waved.

Billy stood and dusted off the back of his jeans.

"I should have known better than to come," he said. "This is worse than gawking at a car wreck." He looked across the river at Luke. "I'm on the wrong side of the river anyway. I'll see you later, Maggie."

Billy made his way back up the ridge as the helicopter rose and vanished over Wolf Cliff.

The sky was silent again, and still mainly blue, but darker clouds pressed in from the north.

Allen stood with Phillips now. I took out the Nikon and photographed Brennon's men in the river drilling, the others assembling portions of the dam. The water continued to clear. First glints of mica came to light, then the white sand, and finally the scuttle of minnows and crayfish and the drift of caddis fly pupas. It was like watching a photograph rinse into clarity.

Luke now watched through a pair of binoculars. The binoculars aimed at Brennon's men then shifted to the bulldozed gash before returning to the river. I had known Luke for eight years, and in that time my feelings toward him had covered the emotional gamut from love to hate. Only now did I feel something close to sorrow.

"PHILLIPS CHECKED IN WITH EARL WILKINSON UP AT THE bridge," Allen said when he sat down. "The river is up to one point nine."

"And they're still going to try?"

"Phillips isn't thrilled, to say the least. I get the feeling if it were his call he'd stop it, but he's getting big-time pressure, and it's evidently coming from the governor on down."

Allen shrugged.

"Who knows. Brennon says it will work, even with the water high."

"I'm not so sure," I said.

The helicopter clattered back over the gorge.

"How long will it take them to put it up?" I asked.

"Two more hours at most. They'll drill seven holes, then bolt the supports together and stretch polyurethane across it. Then the divers go in."

I looked at Randy and Ronny.

"Has Brennon asked the Moseleys what they think about the water level?"

"I doubt it. This is Brennon's dam. I suppose he figures he knows more than anyone else about what it can and can't do."

Allen and I sat down on the shore. He pressed his hand against the back of my neck, his fingers kneading the muscles. I closed my eyes and let my head lean back into his touch.

"That feels good," I said, rolling my head from side to side, the sun warm on my upraised face. The tensions of the last few days broke free and drifted away. "It's obvious Freud never gave a woman a neck rub, else he'd never have asked what a woman wants."

"I see," Allen said. "I'll have to remember that."

I leaned my head in the crevice between Allen's neck and shoulder.

I closed my eyes and must have napped, because when I opened them the drillers had waded out of the water, and seven metal braces rose like submarine periscopes in the water above the falls. I watched Brennon's crew bolt the braces together. All the men wore life jackets and safety ropes. Four worked in the water while the other four held the ropes.

I stood to look more closely at the river. The water was dingy again. I saw Joel on the far bank. He knew as well as I what that dingy water meant.

I looked over at Phillips, the walkie-talkie strapped like a second pistol on his hip, then at Randy and Ronny, who were in their wet suits.

"He may already know it, but I'd better go tell Phillips it's raining upstream," I said.

"You want me to go with you?" Allen asked.

"No, I'll just be a second."

I walked upstream to where Phillips stood with Brennon and Herb Kowalsky.

"It's raining upriver," I said, "probably near the Georgia line."

"We know that," Phillips said. "Earl Wilkinson called a few minutes ago."

"But it's not a real heavy rain," Brennon said, as much as to Phillips as me. "The river may not go down anymore, but it won't go up much either."

"What does Earl say the level is now?"

I was asking Phillips, but Brennon answered. "It's an even two feet. We're still fine."

"I think you'd better postpone this awhile," I said to Phillips.

"This has been decided," Brennon said. "Not by me or Mr. Phillips here but by Superintendent Luckadoo. Nothing can stop that dam from going up now."

"The Tamassee can stop it," I said, and pointed upstream where the big white oak balanced on the boulders. "If it can do that, it can knock down a piece of polyurethane."

I turned to Phillips.

"Luckadoo's lived in the piedmont all his life. He doesn't know anything about white water either. Only the people up here know."

Brennon was a man who had revealed little of himself. I did not know if he was being paid by Kowalsky or had volunteered his time and equipment. I didn't even know if he had children himself. But in the last twelve hours there had been glimpses, first his compassion and now a much less noble attribute—arrogance.

"I keep hearing that," Brennon said, "and it's going to give me a lot of satisfaction when I prove all you self-proclaimed experts wrong."

Phillips didn't speak for a few seconds. His eyes scanning the river's edge, he looked like a man trying to read a language he didn't understand.

"You're positive this dam's going to work," Phillips finally said, his eyes steady on the river.

"Yes, yes, yes," Brennon said. "This is what I do for a living.

I make them and I test them. Do I have to give you a sworn affidavit to be believed?"

"Okay," Phillips said.

"At least make them wait a few hours," I said.

"Why?" Brennon asked. "So we can risk a downpour?" He turned to his men. "Let's get going."

I walked downstream. When I glanced back, Phillips's eyes were still on the river.

I sat down beside Allen and we watched as four of Brennon's crew shouldered the rolled-up polyurethane and waded into the water. When they got midstream they fastened it to the metal and began to work their way back toward shore. The dam unfolded like a huge flag. The river surged against the taut polyurethane, but the first section held. The dam was an A-frame, something I hadn't realized until I saw the middle section unfold.

As Brennon's crew installed the second section, one of the workers slipped. One moment he stood by a metal brace, and the next he hurtled downstream toward Wolf Cliff Falls, his arms flailing for a hold that wasn't there. Suddenly his rope jerked tight. The worker was dragged and jolted across the current toward shore, the man holding the rope now joined by two other men in a tug-of-war with the river. They didn't quit pulling until he lay on a sandbar gasping for breath. He refused to go back in.

Joel had made his way upstream and stood directly across from Randy and Ronny. When he got their attention he shook his head.

"Is he telling them not to go in?" Allen asked.

"Yes, that it's too dangerous."

Brennon's crew worked in shallower water now and their progress quickened. The crowd on the shore became more attentive. Several of the men shouted encouragement. A woman lifted a crying child so it could see better. The teenagers quit splashing each other and watched the men struggle to anchor the last of the polyurethane.

The Kowalskys had been standing away from everyone else. But now they came to the pool's edge. Wearing hiking boots, jeans, and a flannel shirt, Herb Kowalsky had dressed appropriately for the descent into the gorge, but his wife had not. Ellen Kowalsky's sole concession to the terrain was a pair of black Reebok walking shoes, but the incongruity of her mismatched outfit did not lessen her dignity.

She had evidently slipped during the descent, for mud stained her right leg and the side of her dress. She stood with her feet slightly apart, one hand clasping her husband's upper arm as if she too bolstered the final link of the dam.

Water hammered against all three sections of polyurethane. The dam bowed against the pressure as the water rose, but it held.

"It's going to work," Allen said, as I raised my Nikon and took several shots of the completed dam.

The water did as Brennon said it would, diverting into the right side of the river, cutting the flow over Wolf Creek Falls in half.

I moved my head and framed an upstream rock on the far shoreline that had been completely dry half an hour ago. Water rubbed against it now.

"For a little while anyway," I said.

I lowered my camera and looked upstream at Ellen Kowalsky. She had let go of her husband's arm. She faced the pool but her eyes were slightly averted, as though afraid to look directly at the water that held not her daughter but her daughter's remains. I wondered if she had only now begun to realize what she was about to see.

"Do you think she's ready for this?" Allen asked.

"No. Whatever comes out of that pool is going to be worse than anything she could imagine."

I looked at the rock again but couldn't tell if the water had risen any higher.

"She probably should have stayed at her motel," I said.

"Yes," Allen said. "I understand that she has to see the body, but I wish for her sake it could be in a funeral home and in private."

Brennon waved us toward him.

"Come on," Allen said, as he stood up, "they must be getting ready to send a diver in."

I put the Nikon in my backpack before standing up.

"You don't think you'll need that?" Allen asked.

"No," I said, looking at Ellen Kowalsky.

We walked upstream, passing Sheriff Cantrell and Hubert McClure, who were now holding back everyone but the press from the pool. Sheriff Cantrell nodded as I passed. He might not have remembered my first name but he knew who I was because years ago he and Daddy had fished and hunted some together. Sheriff Cantrell had come by our house the week Ben had gotten home from the burn center. He'd given Ben a deputy's badge and told him to heal up quick so they could go catch some bad guys.

It would have been interesting to know which people, if any, Sheriff Cantrell considered the bad guys in this situation. He was too busy watching Luke and the crowd to talk now, but even if he'd had the time I knew he would have kept his thoughts to himself. Although the political pressure wasn't as overt as on Walter Phillips, I suspected Sheriff Cantrell had received his share of e-mails and phone calls from Columbia politicians.

When Brennon gathered everyone he wanted by the pool, he turned to where Randy and Ronny sat on the bank.

"You guys ready?" he asked.

Randy looked at Brennon and shook his head. "We ain't going in. River's too high."

"You're not going in?" Brennon said, his voice incredulous.

Herb Kowalsky moved closer to Brennon. "What?" Kowalsky asked, looking not at the twins but at Brennon. "They're not going in after all this?"

"You've got to go in," Brennon said.

"We ain't got to do nothing," Ronny said.

Randy heaved his oxygen tank toward Brennon. The metal clanged as it hit the ground. Ronny did the same, but aimed his toward Kowalsky.

"There," Randy said. "You two go in if you're so sure it's safe."

The gorge suddenly seemed quieter, even the water. I looked at the dam. The water rose to within a foot of the top. The polyurethane waved and billowed. Joel no longer stood on the far bank. He walked slowly up the trail. Like Billy, he'd evidently seen enough.

"Please," Ellen Kowalsky pleaded. "Please get my daughter out of there."

She opened her palms to Randy as if to say she had nothing to offer but her words.

"Please," she said again. "Please."

Randy stared right at her but didn't speak. I felt Allen's hand settle on my shoulder. It suddenly seemed as if we had all gathered for this one moment. Except moment was the wrong word, because what I felt was an absence of the temporal, as if the mountains had shut us off not only from the rest of the world but from time.

"Don't do it," Ronny said to his twin.

Randy reached out for his tank. "Got to," he said.

Ronny picked up his mask. "I'm going in too," Ronny said.

"No, I need you on shore."

Randy put on his flippers and mask and stepped into the water.

"The rope," Ronny said, and flung one end to his twin.

Randy grabbed the rope and tied a single quick knot as he waded into the pool. He inserted his mouthpiece and leaned into the water. One black fin broke the surface and he was gone.

Walter Phillips's walkie-talkie crackled and I heard Earl Wilkinson's voice announcing the river was at two feet.

"We're still okay," Brennon said, his eyes fixed not on the pool but on the dam. For the first time his voice sounded tentative. "We got a few more minutes."

I looked at the dam. The water was no longer a foot from the top but inches.

I jerked my shoulder free from Allen's hand.

"Get him out," I yelled at Ronny. "Right now."

Ronny turned to us. He stood in the shallows, the rope in his left hand. For a moment I didn't think he heard me. Then he began quickly pulling in the slack.

"Two minutes," Brennon shouted at Ronny. "Give him two more minutes and we'll have her out."

I turned back to the dam, trying to will it to stay up until Randy was out. Something seemed to buckle slightly on both ends, then just as quickly stabilize.

You imagined that, I told myself. It didn't give any.

And then I knew it had.

As the middle section collapsed, the other two folded in like playing cards. A wave broke over Wolf Cliff Falls. People downstream scrambled up banks as an explosion of water surged past. Up on the cliff the river rats didn't yet realize that Randy hadn't gotten out. They began to cheer.

Ronny pulled on the rope, his neck veins bulging as he dug his feet in sand and leaned backward. For a few moments the rope stretched taut between the pool and shore. Then the rope whipped out of the water like a broken fishing line.

Ronny fell backward, landing on his back, his head hitting as well. He got up slowly, sand on his wet suit, his palms seared by rope burns. Then he was stumbling down the river edge shouting for his brother. He searched fifty yards downstream before he turned and ran back toward the pool.

When Luke's group saw the rope they quit cheering. They knew as well as anyone present what it meant. The people downstream realized something terrible had happened as well. The explosion of water had drenched some of them. Knees and elbows had been scraped raw by rocks and sand. Children screamed. A woman clutched her forearm against her stomach. Walter Phillips stood among them, the walkie-talkie pressed to the side of his face as he gave directions to EMS.

Brennon had not moved. He stared where the dam had been as if it were still there and everything he'd just witnessed a mere hallucination. The Kowalskys stood beside him. Herb Kowalsky stared at where the dam had been as well, but his wife's eyes were on the pool. She raised a tissue to the bridge of her nose and wiped away a tear.

"It should have held," Brennon said, more to himself than the Kowalskys. He turned to the Kowalskys. "It should have held," he said again. Only then did Brennon move, sending his men into the shallows to look for Randy. Wading in himself as well.

Allen still stood behind me, but I didn't turn or reach my hand back to grasp his.

Ronny was in the pool's tailwaters, looking for bubbles. There were none, though the white water would have made them hard to see. He ran to where his gear lay and strapped on his tank before Sheriff Cantrell and Hubert McClure pinned him to the ground.

Ellen Kowalsky stepped into the pool, water covering her shoes and rising to her shins. Allen waded out and turned her away from the falls. His hand rested lightly on her elbow as they moved slowly, almost ceremoniously, back to shore. The crumpled tissue fell from her hand. It looked like a dogwood blossom as it drifted toward the pool's center, then sank.

CHAPTER 9

Randy's tank had thirty minutes of oxygen. After forty-five minutes, Sheriff Cantrell told Hubert McClure to unlock the handcuffs on Ronny's wrists.

"Maybe this should have been your call," Cantrell said, turning to Walter Phillips, "but I did what I thought best."

"I've got no problems with that," Phillips said.

"You should have let me try," Ronny screamed, jerking his wrists free from the metal. The cuffs clattered against the rocks at his feet. "Neither one of you had any right to stop me."

"And have three bodies in there?" Sheriff Cantrell said. "No, thanks."

Most everyone had left now. A few reporters lingered, but they were having trouble getting anyone to talk.

"I can't believe this happened," Allen said, breaking the silence between us. Like me, he wanted to believe it hadn't happened, couldn't have happened. He wanted to believe there was still some possibility, no matter how remote, that Randy might yet emerge alive from the pool.

Brennon and his crew had spread the dam's middle section across a sandbar. They studied and pointed as if it were a military map for an upcoming battle. In a way it was, for Brennon was already planning for the next morning. No one but his crew listened. The Kowalskys had gone back to their motel in Seneca. Walter Phillips stood yards away with Ronny and Sheriff Cantrell.

"I need to speak to Phillips a minute," Allen said.

"I'm going to the car," I said.

"I'll just be a minute."

"I can't stay here another minute," I said and made my way across river rocks to the trail end.

The sun had made the ascent less slick than the coming down, but several times I grabbed rhododendron and mountain laurel to keep my balance. The car was unlocked, parked facing a stand of white oak. I got in and stared through the windshield at shapes left by the breeze, the way there was first a space between leaves and then not.

Ten minutes passed and still no sign of Allen. I wrote a note that I was walking back to the motel and left it on the seat. I walked fast, and soon the thin mountain air quickened my breathing. I tripped on a root and turned my ankle but kept going.

I was almost to the blacktop when Allen pulled alongside and opened the passenger door. I kept walking, the open door matching my pace.

"Please get in," he said.

"Why?" I asked.

"Because we're in this together."

Allen put his foot on the brake and waited until I'd sat down and closed the door.

"They're meeting down there at ten tomorrow morning," Allen said, releasing the brake.

"Why?" I asked.

"Brennon is wanting to try again."

"Who does he think he can get into that pool, Ronny? Joel?"

"He's talking about flying some former navy SEAL in from Illinois. Brennon believes he knows what caused the dam to collapse today. He says a few minor adjustments and the dam will be 'viable.' "

"Brennon believes he knows," I said, repeating Allen's words back to him. "And Phillips is going to let him try after what happened today?"

"Who knows the politics of this?" Allen said, frustration in his voice as well. "Who knows what Luckadoo or Senator Jenkins or the damn governor for that matter will tell Phillips to do?"

A half mile up, the two-lane asphalt darkened with recent rain. The tires shushed and whispered.

I spoke only after we parked in the motel lot.

"I'm going to lie down in my room," I told Allen.

"You can do that on my bed."

"No. I want to be alone awhile."

"I'll be in my room," Allen said. "You change your mind, come there."

Allen took my hand and didn't seem to want to let go. I freed myself from his grip.

"We're going to have to talk about this, Maggie," Allen said.

"Not now," I said, and went inside.

I closed the curtains and found an easy-listening station on the radio. I didn't undress, just lay down on the bedsheets and tried not to think. My head hurt, but there were no aspirin in my purse. I did not close my eyes because I knew I would see Randy's flipper disappearing into the pool.

The radio did no good so I turned it off.

Think about something else besides today, I told myself, and I cast my memory out like a fishing line.

I was eight years old. Ben and I wore our Sunday clothes, though it was a Thursday afternoon. We were at our Grandfather Holcombe's farm. He was in heaven, the grown-ups said, though Ben and I knew better because we'd peeked in the box. When we'd eaten our fill of fried chicken and banana pudding, we sneaked off from the adults and went down to the bridge that crossed Licklog Creek. We lay on the gray splintery boards, our foreheads pressed to the slats. Water spiders skimmed the surface as salamanders bellied across the sandy bottom. A snake unspooled on the bank and crossed the pool before disappearing into a clump of reeds.

My grandfather is dead, I had thought to myself as I looked into the pool, then whispered the same words as my mouth pressed against the wood.

And now, twenty years later, I remembered something I had forgotten—my father stepping through the barbed wire in his suit. Ben and I expected to be punished, since we'd been warned never to go near streams or ponds without a grown-up.

"You all know better than to come down here alone," Daddy said, but his words were gentle. "It would near about kill your daddy if one of his babies was to get hurt." He'd lifted us up into his arms and walked upstream to the cow guard and then to the truck where Momma waited.

I LAY ON THE BED A FEW MORE MINUTES BEFORE I GOT UP AND showered. I let hot water beat against my neck and back till the bathroom became a sauna. I felt the sweat bead all over my body like another layer of skin. I didn't want to leave that shower, but after twenty minutes the water began to cool. I got dressed and went to Allen's room.

The door was unlocked. Allen lay on his bed, the only light coming through the gap in the curtains. As my eyes adjusted to the darkness I saw a lampshade on the floor, jagged pieces of the lamp itself scattered close by.

I looked outside and saw the late-afternoon sky was cloudless. If they could have just waited a day, maybe just a few hours, I thought.

I closed the curtain and lay down beside Allen.

"Some of those children in the café," Allen said. "They were his children, weren't they?"

"Yes. A girl and a boy."

Allen pressed the back of his hand to his forehead, as if shielding his face from a blow.

"How old are they?" he asked, his voice slightly muffled by his forearm.

"Sheila's four. Gary is seven."

"If I could have even imagined it could turn out this way. . . ."

"You couldn't," I said. "But I'm not so sure I can say that for myself. Joel knew it could happen, and Randy and Ronny knew too. What they knew I should have known, did know."

"You warned them," Allen said.

"I warned them too late."

Allen put his arm under my neck and turned me toward him. "He was a good father to those children, wasn't he?"

"From everything I know, yes, he was."

"A better father than I was," Allen said. He pulled me closer.

We pressed ourselves against each other, into each other. For a moment I thought of undressing, of putting my hand on the back of Allen's head and leading his mouth to my flesh.

But I also thought of what it would feel like afterward— the smell of sex on our bodies, tangled sheets, late-afternoon light slanting through the window.

Perhaps we might transcend everything that had happened that day, and there might be enough lingering afterward to hearten us through the rest of the day and night. But there was also the possibility that the temporary distraction would be just that—temporary—and so much the sadder for its transience. Then the room would only feel emptier, the space between Allen and me, between ourselves and our own hearts, wider.

I wasn't ready for us to take that risk, not yet.

I kissed Allen lightly on the mouth.

"I need to go," I said.

"Don't," Allen said, then mashed his lips roughly against mine. His fingers tried to loosen the metal button on my jeans. I jerked my mouth free from his.

"No," I said, in a harsh tone. I laid my palms against Allen's chest and pushed. Like a puppet suddenly unstrung, his whole body gave way. He rolled on his back.

"Oh, God. I'm sorry, Maggie," he whispered.

I rubbed a finger across my upper lip. No blood, but it would be swollen. I got off the bed. For a few moments I stood there hoping one of us might find some word or gesture that would make things right again. But none came.

I walked over to the door and put my hand on the knob. I let go and turned toward the bed.

"Are you going to the meeting tomorrow?"

"Yes," he said. "Why not? I've seen it through this far. I owe it to someone, I'm just not sure who."

"I'll go with you," I said.

I looked out the window a last time, the sun lower in the sky but the sky still blue. Just a few more hours.

"Do you want me to open the curtains?"

"No," Allen said. "Leave them closed."

• • •

I DID NOT GO BACK TO MY ROOM. INSTEAD, I LEFT THE MOTEL
and walked the half mile to Billy's store. I stepped onto the
porch and opened the screen door. Wanda sat on a stool
behind the counter. The boys knelt beside the drink box
building a cabin with Lincoln logs.

"Maggie," Wanda said when I came in. It was a perfunctory
greeting.

I crossed the store to the second row of shelves and picked
up a bottle of aspirin.

"One forty-eight," Wanda said when I placed the bottle on
the counter. She took the dollar bills from my hand without
looking at me and opened the cash register.

"Where's Billy tonight?" I asked.

Wanda looked at me then. "He's gone over to see Jill Moseley and the children. See if there's anything he can do for
them."

The boys heard the harshness in their mother's voice. They
stopped building and looked up at her, then at me.

"You know of anything I can do to help out?"

"No," Wanda said. "We'll do what can be done."

The register made a clapping sound as Wanda shoved it
closed.

"This ain't Columbia," Wanda said. "We still look after
our own."

"I grew up here," I said. "I know that."

Wanda checked to make sure the boys had resumed playing. "Then you know what I mean when I say we look after

our own. We look after our neighbors before we look after people who come here and tell us to our faces we're stupid hillbillies. We look after our own fathers before we worry about the father of someone we've never met."

Wanda gave me my change, dropping it in my hand so our flesh didn't touch.

"Goodbye, Wanda," I said.

I walked back to the room and took two aspirin, then picked up the phone. He answered on the third ring.

"You've heard about Randy, I guess."

"Yes, Margaret called me," Daddy said, his voice guarded.

"I was there when it happened."

"I know that too."

Daddy paused. A vacuum cleaner roared to life in the hall outside my door, and I cupped the receiver closer to my ear.

"Margaret said Reverend Tilson will have a service of sorts on the river come morning."

"Where on the river?" I asked.

"There at Wolf Cliff."

"That's not an easy place to get to, even after the bulldozers," I said. "And it's slippery."

"Randy's momma and wife want it there. I reckon Reverend Tilson feels he's got to do what they ask. I'd go if I thought I could walk back out once I got down in there, but that chemotherapy's taken the starch out of me."

"You're feeling worse?" I asked.

"No worse than what the doctors said I'd feel. It ain't nothing I wasn't expecting."

In my mind I followed the telephone lines up Highway 76

and through pasture and orchard edge, down Damascus Church Road, then across the pasture to where my father sat in his front room, the glassed photographs of his wife and children staring down on him.

"About last week," I said, and paused. What I wanted to say was I was sorry, sorry for a lot of things.

But the words wouldn't come. Because I was imagining how Wanda or Jill Moseley would react to my words, how they'd be justified in saying it was a damn convenient time for me to be so suddenly forgiving. Daddy could say much the same.

"You told me what you believed," he said, petulance sharpening his voice. "You got what you think of me out in the open."

The vacuum cleaner shut off. I could hear it being rolled farther up the hall.

"I want things better between us," I said.

"You haven't much acted like it," Daddy said. "That's what I've been trying to do ever since you been up here."

Anger sparked inside me for a moment but didn't catch. I was too weary to nurture it.

"I'm going to try harder," I said.

Daddy said nothing for a few moments. "I'm sorry you were there today," he said. "I'd have wished it otherwise."

"I know that," I said, and told him good night.

I slept that night, more than I thought possible. I woke once and the radio clock glowed two-twenty. I wondered if Allen was awake. I thought how nice it would be if I were lying with his chest pressed into my back, his knees tucked behind mine. A breeze ruffled the curtains. Crickets and tree frogs gave voice to the weeds and branches. I'd often had trouble sleeping well in Laurens and Columbia and always assumed the reason was the sound of cars passing, neighbors shutting doors and dragging trash cans to the curb, but now I realized it was also what I didn't hear—rain on a tin roof, crickets, tree frogs, owls, whippoorwills—sounds so much a part of the night you didn't even notice them until they were absent.

I thought about the words I'd almost said to Daddy. "What can be spoken is already dead in the heart," Luke had often said. Nietzsche. I didn't believe that was always true. But words could be easy, mere movements of the mouth. As I lay there trying to articulate what I felt toward Daddy, toward myself, the words rang hollow—hollow and self-serving.

Eventually I sank back into sleep. I dreamed of a face staring up at me from the bottom of the pool at Wolf Creek Falls. The water was murky but it slowly began to clear, the face becoming more and more familiar.

REVEREND TILSON HAD AGED SINCE I'D SEEN HIM LAST, IN large part because of the heart attack he'd suffered in December. New lines creased his face. The slump in his shoulders was more pronounced. He had been an energetic man who rarely stayed behind the pulpit when he preached. Instead, he'd roamed the aisles, Bible in hand, still only when reading a passage. On summer Sundays he wore no suit or tie but preached in a white short-sleeve dress shirt and his one suit's black pants. Sweat soaked his shirt, sticking to his skin like gauze to a wound. When I was twelve he carried me in his arms into the Tamassee. I had felt his biceps tense against my back as he'd eased me into the water.

"You're a child of God now," he told me, as I'd come sputtering out of the water, "and ever always you will be."

Now, sixteen years later, he paused between each step as if uncertain the ground would support him. His son helped him down the trail to where the rest of the congregation gathered on the shore below Wolf Cliff Falls, but once on the bank he walked alone to the water's edge. He turned his back to the falls and faced his congregation.

At the angle where I stood, I recognized faces I'd known since childhood, some of them belonging to relatives. Some returned my gaze, and their eyes made it clear they knew I'd played a role in their gathering here this morning. Jill Moseley and her mother-in-law stood in the center, the rest of the church members huddled around them. Only Ronny did not wear his church clothes, dressed instead in a black T-shirt, jeans, and tennis shoes. His children were not present, nor were Randy's.

Upstream, Sheriff Cantrell and Walter Phillips stood where the dam had been built. To the left of Sheriff Cantrell lay Ronny's wet suit, tank, and flippers. Up on the ridge across the river, Luke sat by himself. He wore what he'd worn yesterday. I knew he, like Hubert McClure, had stayed here all night.

Reverend Tilson bowed his head.

"Lord, hear our prayers this morning. Let not our hearts be troubled in this trying time," he said, his voice still strong.

"Let us know you are with us this morning, Lord, in our time of trial. Amen."

"Amen," the congregation echoed.

Reverend Tilson raised his head.

"Let us pray individually now. Let the Lord know our hearts, our needs at this troubled time. Any so moved speak now."

"I'll be back in a few minutes," I told Allen, and lifted up my backpack. I walked up the trail as Agnes Moseley prayed for her son's soul.

I soon left the trail and made my way to the cave. I clicked on the flashlight as I entered and felt again its cool moistness. I swept the light in front of my feet and in a few minutes came to the campfire. Beside it lay marbles and a toy train Aunt Margaret had bought Ben when he was still in the hospital. Soft drink cans and candy wrappers lay on the cave floor as well.

And a paint set, left open, a brush lying beside it. I shined the light on the cave wall.

The stick figure was still on the wall, but now three other ones had joined it, one the same size and two larger. Their arms too were upraised. The face of the original figure was now smudged black, not by paint but ashes. The second figure was smudged as well, not on the face but on one arm and one leg. The larger figures were unmarked but one arm of each connected to an arm of a smaller figure. All four faces looked upward, and tears of white paint fell from their eyes.

I sat down on the floor. I cut off the flashlight and put my head on my knees. I didn't want to see or be seen.

After a while I got up and walked back down to the river. The last of the individual prayers were being offered when I rejoined Allen.

"Sister Lusk, will you sing for us?" Reverend Tilson said when no one else raised a hand to pray.

Aunt Margaret nodded and took a step forward. Hours spent in her garden had tanned her arms and face. She seemed to have grown stronger with age. She and my father looked less alike now than any time in their lives. But her eyes were my father's eyes, the same shade of blue. My eyes as well.

She had sung at tent revivals and weddings and funerals since her teen years and had accepted invitations to sing as far away as West Virginia. In 1985 the Smithsonian had recorded her for its folksingers collection. But Aunt Margaret always said singing for family and friends was what meant the most to her.

She looked my way and nodded, her face as open and generous as it had always been. She began to sing.

Shall we gather at the river,
Where bright angel feet have trod,
With its crystal tide forever
Flowing by the throne of God?

Yes, we'll gather at the river,
The beautiful, the beautiful river;
Gather with the saints at the river
That flows by the throne of God.

On the ridge above me I heard voices. Through the trees I saw Brennon and his crew bringing down their equipment. Herb Kowalsky trailed them. His wife was not with him but a man carrying an oxygen tank and duffel bag was. On the other side Luke no longer sat alone. Carolyn and several others had joined him.

Soon we'll reach the shining river.
Soon our pilgrimage will cease.

My aunt's voice echoed off Wolf Cliff. I looked at Ronny and tried to remember the last time I'd seen him without his brother beside him.

Yes, we'll gather at the river,
The beautiful, the beautiful river;
Gather with the saints at the river
That flows by the throne of God.

"Thank you, Sister Lusk," Reverend Tilson said, as Brennon's crew dropped what they'd carried on the shore. Brennon led his men back up the trail to get the rest of the equipment, leaving Kowalsky and the diver behind.

Walter Phillips stepped closer to the trail.

"Mr. Brennon," Phillips said, but Brennon did not turn around. "We haven't had our meeting yet, Mr. Brennon," Phillips said. "Nobody's going to do anything until I'm positive what happened yesterday can't happen again."

Brennon turned. "You heard what Luckadoo said on the

phone last night," he said, and continued up the trail, his men following. Kowalsky and the diver did not join Sheriff Cantrell and Phillips but stayed at the trailhead.

When the gorge grew quiet again, Reverend Tilson opened a tattered Bible bound by black electrician's tape.

"The word of the Lord," he said, and began to read.

" 'Behold, there was a great earthquake: for the angel of the Lord descended from heaven, and came and rolled back the stone from the door, and sat upon it. His countenance was like lightning, and his rainment white as snow. And for fear of him the keepers did shake, and became as dead men. And the angel answered and said unto the women, Fear ye not: for I know that ye seek Jesus, which was crucified. He is not here: for he is risen.' "

Reverend Tilson closed his Bible. He stepped into the shallows until water rose to his calves.

"Christ rose that we all might rise," he said, waving the Bible over the water. "Randy Moseley, our brother in Christ, may be in that river, but if God wills it he will rise from it this morning and be among us."

Jill Moseley held on to Ronny's arm as she slowly pressed her knees into the sand one at a time. Others knelt as well.

"Raise him, Lord," Wallace Eller shouted.

Allen leaned toward me, his hand pressing my arm. "Do they really believe their prayers can resurrect him?"

"Yes," I said. "They do."

"Raise his soul, Lord," Reverend Tilson shouted, "as you have promised. And we would ask more, Lord, for you to raise his body from this river so his family may see him a last time."

"Please, Lord," Jill Moseley prayed, eyes closed, voice fervent. Her face and arms were uplifted, and the late-morning sun lay like a palm of light across her forehead.

"He was baptized in this river, Lord," Reverend Tilson said. The old man stooped so the fingers of his left hand touched the water that swirled over his ankles. "I've lifted him from this river in my own arms and in Thy name. I'm too old to lift him, Lord. You must lift him from these waters now."

Reverend Tilson pointed his dripping hand toward the hydraulic. "And this child who lies with him, given the name Ruth by her parents, a Godly name, Lord. Raise her too, body and soul into the light." Everyone in the congregation knelt now except Ronny and Reverend Tilson.

I knelt as well. Allen hesitated, then pressed his knees into the sand beside me.

"Hear our prayers, Lord," Reverend Tilson said, "as we make our individual petitions to You on this riverbank. Hear us, Lord. Amen."

"Amen," the congregation answered, and dispersed into groups of three and four to kneel together and hold hands, their prayers blending with the sound of the river. Allen helped me to my feet.

Ronny walked upstream, neither nodding nor speaking as he passed in front of Allen and me. He didn't speak to anyone else, either. He found a spot between Kowalsky and Phillips. Ronny crouched, not as though to pray but as he would in his orchard, hips touching the backs of his calves but not the ground while he rocked slightly on his heels.

"What's he doing?" Allen asked.

"Making sure he's part of whatever is going to happen," I said.

In a few minutes Brennon and his men came back down the trail with the remainder of their equipment. Kowalsky and the diver joined them, as did Sheriff Cantrell and Ronny and Walter Phillips.

"So what do you want to meet about?" Brennon asked Phillips, not looking at Phillips as he spoke but at his men checking the equipment.

Walter Phillips looked weary beyond his years. If he'd slept at all last night it had been very little. I wondered if what had kept him awake was frustration, stress, or, perhaps, guilt. Maybe he had someone he could confide in, a close friend or relative, but that person was not in Oconee County. This morning he was seemingly alone.

"I want to know why I should believe this dam of yours will work any better today than it did yesterday," Walter Phillips asked.

"The water's lower today," Brennon answered brusquely. "Wilkinson said it's down to one point five." He gestured toward the river. "Look how clear it is compared to yesterday."

"If that dam can't hold up at one point eight," Phillips asked, "why should I believe it can hold up at one point five?"

"We're wasting time here," Brennon said. "It may start raining again."

"We're not rushing this," Phillips said, and as he spoke I looked at his hands and saw they were clinched as they'd been in my photograph. His shoulders seemed to widen slightly, his stomach tightening as if preparing to receive a blow. Or maybe deliver one.

"He puts it up, I'll go in," Ronny said and pointed to Brennon's diver. "He don't have to go. It's my brother in there. I'll take the risk."

"I'm not afraid to try it," Brennon's diver said, as much to Ronny as Phillips.

"Then we'll both go in," Ronny said.

Walter Phillips spoke softly, so softly no one seemed at first to understand what he had said.

"What did you say?" Herb Kowalsky asked.

"I said nobody's going in. That dam's not going up, not until I've got good reason to believe it will hold."

"You can't do this," Brennon said. His face flushed with anger. "You heard what Luckadoo said last night. He said if I was confident the dam would work to go ahead. He didn't say you. He said me."

"Luckadoo isn't here," Walter Phillips said. "This is going to be my call."

At that moment I knew Walter Phillips might well be kissing whatever career he hoped to have with the Forest Service goodbye. I suspected he understood this as well, and tomorrow or ten or thirty years from now he could conceivably look back with regret on this moment.

"You can't do this," Herb Kowalsky said, but the dejected tone in his voice argued that he knew Phillips could. And had.

Brennon looked at his men for a moment. They had stopped unpacking equipment. Their eyes were on their employer, waiting for instructions.

Brennon turned his gaze back to Phillips.

"What if we go ahead and decide we're going to build that dam anyway? What are going to do about it?"

"Stop you," Walter Phillips said.

I looked at the polished black holster on his hip. Walter Phillips had probably taken his gun from that holster a few times on the job. He looked at Brennon, and his eyes, like his voice, revealed no fear or even nervousness, only resolve.

Brennon turned to Sheriff Cantrell.

"Whose side are you on?"

Sheriff Cantrell nodded at Phillips.

"His."

Sheriff Cantrell raised his voice so Brennon's crew could hear him. "And so is my deputy. If one of your men so much as dips his toe in that river I'll lock him and you both up."

"You've no right to do this, Sheriff," Herb Kowalsky said, "no more right than Phillips does."

"I'll worry about what rights I got, Mr. Kowalsky," Sheriff Cantrell said. "I'm sorry about your daughter, I really am, but one man has already died trying to get her out. I'll not let that river kill another."

"This is going to cost you your job," Brennon said to Sheriff Cantrell.

Sheriff Cantrell smiled at Brennon.

"Sheriff's an elected office in Oconee County, Mr. Brennon, and we don't tend to get many write-in votes from Illinois."

"I'm calling Luckadoo soon as I get back to the motel," Brennon said. He motioned to his men to begin picking up the gear.

I waited for Kowalsky to make further threats himself, but the face he'd worn at the meetings and on the river fell away like a discarded mask. He looked like his wife when she'd spoken at the community center. Something had broken inside him now as well, or maybe, up until now, he'd just been able to hide that break beneath his anger and indignation. He did not follow Brennon and his crew up the trail. Instead, he walked ten yards downstream and sat on a rock. I wondered if he was pondering what he would tell his wife. Or perhaps merely delaying those words a few minutes longer.

Ronny started walking upstream.

"You best leave that diving equipment where it is, Ronny," Sheriff Cantrell said. "I'm going to hold on to it for a few days."

Ronny did not acknowledge Sheriff Cantrell's words, but he didn't try to pick up his diving gear either. He was walking toward Reverend Tilson's service when he suddenly turned and backtracked to the trail. He followed the last of Brennon's men up the ridge.

"Where do you think he's going?" Phillips asked.

"I don't know," Sheriff Cantrell said, "but the farther from here the better."

Reverend Tilson and his congregation continued to pray in groups of three and four. The murmur of prayers merged with the sound of the river. It's Sunday morning, I thought, as though somehow I'd not realized that. Sunday morning in a place where it meant more than sleeping late and a leisurely read of the Sunday paper.

Sunlight poured into the gorge now, warming the rocks,

brightening the river. Yellow mayflies swirled over the pool below Wolf Cliff Falls, the females dipping occasionally to lay their eggs. A trout broke the pool's surface. In the woods behind me a pileated woodpecker tapped a tree trunk as if sending a coded message. The morning felt like spring in a way the previous days here had not. The Tamassee and its banks seemed more alive, busier. I looked at the rhododendron and mountain laurel. They would blossom soon and the flowers would overwhelm the banks with their intense whites and pinks.

Herb Kowalsky still sat on the rock farther upstream. He looked diminished. He was not a likable man, and he must have been a hard man to work for, maybe to live with as well, but at that moment I wanted to be more generous to him. I wanted to believe that he had been as attentive to his daughter in life as in death. I wanted him to have that—despite whatever sorrow or guilt he felt—to know beyond any doubt he had been a good father to his daughter.

Allen reached his arm around my waist.

"Phillips is doing the right thing."

"Yes, he is," I said. "I just hope his superiors see it that way."

"What will happen now?"

"That depends on whether Phillips gets any backing. Come July the river will be more rock than water. They shouldn't have any trouble getting into the undercut then."

"You think they'll be willing to wait that long?"

"I don't know."

Someone was coming down the trail, moving quickly. I turned around, expecting Brennon or one of his crew, but it was Ronny, a backpack slung over his shoulder. He cut off the trail and shoved through mountain laurel till he reached the tailwaters of the pool.

"What are you doing, son?" Reverend Tilson asked, as Ronny waded into the shallows. Reverend Tilson took a few tentative steps after him. "What are you doing, son?" he repeated.

"Get out of there, Moseley," Sheriff Cantrell shouted.

No one moved as Ronny opened the backpack and pulled out three sticks of dynamite, gray masking tape binding them together like a bouquet.

Luke reacted first, running down the ridge as Ronny flared a cigarette lighter. It took him three tries to light the fuse. Sheriff Cantrell and Walter Phillips and Hubert McClure stood at the pool edge now, but they didn't enter the water.

"Don't do it," Sheriff Cantrell said.

"It's what has to be done," Ronny said, and waded deeper into the pool, raising the dynamite in his left hand as the water rose to his chest.

Reverend Tilson raised his hand as though to make a pronouncement as Luke crashed through the last thicket of mountain laurel and onto the rocks at the pool's edge. Like the rest of us he could only watch as Ronny heaved the dynamite into the right side of the falls.

Ronny turned and started wading out as Sheriff Cantrell and Walter Phillips backed away from the pool. Allen tried to pull me toward the woods, but I refused to move.

"Turn your head," Allen shouted at me, but my eyes were on Luke. He'd dived into the pool and was swimming underwater toward the falls. He was going after the dynamite. Maybe to snuff the fuse. Maybe to use his body to shield the river.

Everything was quiet, so quiet I thought I could hear the fuse sizzling under the water.

Then the ground beneath my feet shook and the pool heaved upward like a geyser.

Reverend Tilson stood in the shallows, his white shirt drenched. One of the women in his congregation screamed. The back of Ronny's neck was bleeding. Sheriff Cantrell and Walter Phillips took him by the arms and set him down on a sandbar.

Walter Phillips knelt beside Sheriff Cantrell, blocking my view.

"How bad is it?" he asked.

"I think he's okay," Sheriff Cantrell said.

Luke was staggering back to the opposite shore, his face bloody.

Reverend Tilson was still in the shallows, his hand still upraised. He stared at something in the pool.

"Oh, God," Herb Kowalsky said.

Then I saw what they saw, Randy's and Ruth's bodies rising from the pool's depths into the light.

CHAPTER 10

After death, everything in a house appears slightly transformed—the color of a vase, the length of a bed, the weight of a glass lifted from a cupboard. No matter how many blinds are raised and lamps turned on, light is dimmer. Shadows that cobweb corners spread and thicken. Clocks tick a little louder, the silence between seconds longer. The house itself feels off-plumb, as though its foundation had been calibrated to the weight and movement of the deceased.

So it seems to me on this October afternoon as I box up my father's clothes. Everything and everyone else has been dealt with: the horse and the cow given to Joel; the truck donated to Luke's Forest Watch Project; paperwork done at the courthouse, pictures and a few other heirlooms I'm taking with me packed in the Toyota's trunk; Tony Bryan, who wrongly assumed that Ben and I planned to sell.

After two months I am returning to Columbia.

"Don't worry about your job," Lee had assured me in August. "It'll be here. You take care of your father."

And so I had, in this room where I had emptied bedpans and urinals instead of drawers, lifted pain pills and cough syrup to his mouth and what food and liquid he could swallow, bathed him with a sponge and washtub and afterward rubbed Desitin into his skin. The window is open, as it has been most of the last week, but the smell of stale sweat and urine lingers.

Only a portion of what's in the drawers is worth giving to Goodwill. Some jeans and work pants, some blue socks and a white dress shirt still wrapped in cellophane, two sweaters, a couple of belts. That's it. The T-shirts stained gray with sweat, socks and overalls frayed at heels and knees, underwear and handkerchiefs—all these will be put in a dumpster.

I carry the two boxes out to the car. I shove them into the backseat, turn and gaze across the pasture to Damascus Pentecostal Church, the snaggled rows of stone rising beside it. The grave is easy to spot, an unseasonable blossom of flowers set among a swell of black dirt. A grave dug by Joel and Billy, because, as Wanda Watson once reminded me, "we take care of our own up here."

I hear a crackling of gravel and see Aunt Margaret walking up the drive, one hand clutching a shawl around her neck, in the other a dead man's mail.

"You need something besides a T-shirt on, girl," she says. "It's October, not July."

I nod at the house.

"I've been inside. Anyway, filling and hauling these boxes is enough work to keep me warm."

Aunt Margaret hands me the mail.

"Nothing but advertisements far as I can tell," she says, as I stuff it in the pocket of my jeans. "I got my chores done, so thought I might could help you."

"I'm about done," I say. "One more box load and I'll be on my way."

"When will you be back?"

"Not before Thanksgiving. I've got some serious catching up to do at work."

Aunt Margaret meets my eyes. "What about in the romance department? You got some catching up there as well?"

"Maybe," I say, smiling. "Let's just say I still like the smell of him."

She smiles too. "That's more than just some old wives' tale, girl. There's a whole lot of worse ways to measure a man."

Aunt Margaret looks at the house and lets her gaze linger a few moments. I wonder if, like me, it seems somehow different now. When she turns back to me, tears dampen her cheeks.

"I'll say my goodbye now," she says, "so you can say your own."

Aunt Margaret pulls me to her. I smell the Ivory soap she bathes with, the talcum powder she brushes on her skin each morning and night. She holds me hard, like she wants to remember exactly how I feel, make an imprint of my body on hers. She knows that though she's in as good health as an eighty-two-year-old woman can expect, at her age each good-bye may be the last. She loosens her hold, though her hands linger on my arms a few moments longer.

"Take good care of yourself, Maggie," she says, reaching into her skirt pocket and pulling out a wad of tissue. "I best go now before I make a scene."

She heads back down the drive, dabbing her eyes with the tissue as she walks.

I go back inside, to fill one more cardboard box with my father's clothes, to say my goodbyes, to close more than just this house before I leave. But it isn't that easy. I would like to say my father and I reconciled in these last months, that as I tended him the past was simply forgotten. But there were times the old grievances resurfaced and the less angelic part of our natures won out. When that happened it was easy enough to believe nothing had really changed between us.

Yet it had. We'd made our tentative, sideways gestures of reconciliation, and they were not always self-serving and they were not always futile. Maybe that was as much as we were capable of, especially in a place where even land turns inward, shuts itself off from the rest of the world.

All that's left is the closet. I open its door and smell moth-balls and the dank, musty odor of clothes shut years in dark-ness. The faint linger of cigarette smoke as well. I free cotton and flannel shirts from the rattling jumble of clothes hangers, then dig deeper into the closet for two pair of khaki pants, a heavy winter coat, and a denim work jacket. I stuff them in the cardboard box, then take out the denim jacket and put it on. I stand before the bureau mirror. The sleeves come to my knuckles, the denim loose on my shoulders. Not a good fit, but that seems appropriate. I turn back the sleeves, then lift the last box and carry it outside.

The morning has a cool, clean feel as I drive out Damascus Church Road, and an October sky widens overhead with not a wisp of gray or white cloud, just blue smoothed out like a quilt tacked on a frame. It's a sky that makes everything beneath it brighter, more clarified. I cross the creek and pass bottomland Joel planted in the spring with corn. What stalks remain standing look like something after fire, brittle and singed to an ashy gray, the shriveled shucks clinched close.

The land rises again and I pass Aunt Margaret's house and the church, a pasture, and another cornfield. Then it is only apple orchards, late in the picking season but still some fruit left to dab some red and yellow onto the brown branches. The spring's heavy rains, the rains that had brought me up here in May, have ensured a good harvest.

At the stop sign I turn left, because there is one more place to go before leaving. I pass Billy's store and Luke's cabin, following the land as it leans toward the river. I park on the road's shoulder and walk out until I am at the center of the bridge.

I place my hands on the railing and look down. Poplars and sweet gums hold clutches of gold and purple, but many leaves have already fallen. The thinning foliage makes the river seem wider, as if the banks have been pushed back a few yards on each side. Enough color remains for a good photograph. My camera is in the front seat of my car, but I let it remain there.

The Tamassee is shallow. Rocks underwater in May now jut above the surface. What was once white water flows slow and clear. Two trout waver in the sandy shallows. Their fins break the surface as they drift a few feet downstream then scuttle back to where the female has used her caudal fin to dig a nest. I can see only their black backs, not the blood-red spots on their flanks or the buttermilk yellow of their bellies.

I hear voices from under the bridge, and in a few moments a yellow raft appears, PROPERTY OF TAMASSEE RIVER TOURS stenciled in black on the side. It's late in the year for a rafting trip, probably some business or church group with enough money to talk Earl Wilkinson into pulling a raft out of storage. They wear yellow life jackets and red, green, and blue helmets. One of the rafters sees me and waves. Earl looks up and our eyes meet. He nods but does not smile. I watch the raft scrape and slide downstream, then through Deep Sluice and past Bobcat Rock. The sun is out and the bright colors refract and merge as I offer a kind of prayer.

A breeze lifts off the river. I raise the jacket's collar and tuck the denim lapels under my chin. In another month all the leaves will be shed. Things hidden will emerge: knotholes and barked stretches of root, mistletoe and squirrel nests in the trees' higher junctions. From this bridge I will be able to follow several of the river's bends and curves as it makes a boundary between two states. Outcrops and rivulets will become more visible. Wildlife as well, mainly deer and wild turkeys but also an occasional wild boar or bobcat, even a black bear foraging for mast. Possibly a bigger cat, allowing a glimpse of yellow eyes, a long black-tipped tail, before vanishing back into the realm of faith.

From this bridge I cannot see the pool below Wolf Cliff, but I know the water is low and clear, the shallows thickened by red and yellow and purple leaves. Perhaps trout spawn in those shallows, their fins stirring the leaves as they follow old urgings.

In the boulder-domed dark below the falls, no current slows or curves in acknowledgment of Ruth Kowalsky and Randy Moseley's once-presence, for they are now and forever lost in the river's vast and generous unremembering.

ACKNOWLEDGMENTS

The author wishes to thank John Lane, Marlin Barton, Tom Rash, and Butch Clay for their help with this novel. Special thanks also to Lee Smith, Robert Morgan, Janette Turner Hospital, Silas House, George Singleton, Frye Gaillard, Amy Rogers, Linda Elliott, and Don Garrison. Good people all. I am especially indebted to three angels of the literary realm: Nancy Olson, bookseller extraordinare; Jennifer Barth, as gifted an editor as any writer could hope for; and, most of all, Marly Rusoff, who is not only an exceptional agent but also an exceptional human being. Thank you all.

ABOUT THE AUTHOR

Winner of an NEA poetry fellowship, RON RASH has published three collections of poetry and two of short stories. The paperback edition of his first novel, *One Foot in Eden*, was published by Picador in February 2004. He holds the John Parris Chair in Appalachian Studies at Western Carolina University.